What's Your Problem, Cowboy?

SAM WELCH

What's Your Problem, Cowboy?

by Sam Welch

Table of Contents

Prologue
(Planetary Research and Launch Facility, Nevada, 2025)

The well lit grounds of the Planetary Research and Launch Facility were quiet, with the exception of the distant coyote, hoot owl, and the occasional *zap* when a misguided desert hare ran headlong into the electric wires of the tall cyclone fence.

At one end of the eighty acre compound was the Bone Yard, so named because of the equipment scattered about, rockets, satellite parts, space probes, solid rocket boosters, and components for various stages of flight. Most of it was old and obsolete, saved because ailing budgets and cutbacks required frugality.

Stately buildings of concrete and brick lined the opposite side of the compound. The buildings ranged from three to five stories, all light tan with flat roofs and steel stairwells. Trimmed hedges and white walkways bordered well watered lawns, neatly mowed and edged.

In the center of the compound, under lighting as bright as day, a thirty foot rocket sat on a platform ready for the morning launch.

Day shift had been downsized, night shift was nonexistent except for a part time janitor and the security guard, Stearns, or P.B.J as he was called because of his love for peanut butter and jelly sandwiches. Seeing him without one was like seeing a redneck without a skoal ring on the back pocket of a pair of blue jeans. Stearns watched ten surveillance monitors from an office within the command building. He was a middle aged, overweight and sloppy in more than just appearance. The only thing he loved more than peanut butter and jelly were old western movies.

During graveyard hours he snacked to his heart's content and nobody cared except the janitor who cleaned jelly stains from the shiny tile floors.

One night when the janitor was away, Stearns inserted a disk containing a medley of classic western movies into the diskdrive and watched as the first movie opened on the center monitor. It was a hard riding, guns-blazing flick with plenty of drinking and gambling, a hanging, and a duel at high noon.

Halfway through the first movie, Stearns' thoughts drifted as he nodded away to the dusty streets of Dodge City. He envisioned himself the town marshal facing three villains, dark clad, and poorly shaven. The rhinestones on Stearn's leather vest glistened in the sun, his stiff chaps girded his hips and legs like body armor, and his white ten gallon hat made him seem eight feet tall. His enemies were within range, right where he wanted them. The jingling of his spurs ceased as he came to a stop.

Stearns cocked his head and raised one eyebrow. He popped the knuckles on both hands and readied them above his six guns. The villains, three abreast, seemed equally ready. For a moment a tense silence filled the air, then each man reached for his gun, and the ear shattering sound, as though magnified a thousand times awakened Stearns and brought him upright in his chair. The sound was not a gun blast but the clang of a steel door in the outer passageway. Stearn's eyes fastened on the monitor. A saloon scene was approaching the climax. He wanted to watch but concern for his job overruled his obsession. He ejected the disk from the diskdrive. The monitors came on line. One of them showed a tall slim gentleman in a gray suit and tie using his security badge to enter through the outer scanner points. It was Mr. Kramer, Director of Planetary Research. Stearns sprang to his feet next to the monitor table. He turned to face the door holding the disk behind him with trembling hand.

Kramer entered carrying a briefcase. "Good morning Stearns."

Stearns' eyes widened. He forced a nervous, "good morning sir," and cleared his throat.

Kramer set the briefcase near Stearn's feet, and made his way to the coffee machine.

Stearns tried to sound natural. "What-what brings you in so early, Mr. Kramer?"

Kramer poured coffee into a styrofoam cup. "I just came in to load the video disks into the capsule for this morning's launch."

"Video disks?" Stearns fumbled the D.V.D. which fell to the floor beside Kramer's briefcase. *Kramer must not see it!* Stearn's thoughts were so loud, as he leaned to recover the disk, that he feared Kramer, already returning with his coffee, might overhear him.

Inches shy of the disk, Stearns jerked himself upright and pretended to stretch.

Stooping for his briefcase, Kramer answered, "We're sending a probe with a friendship capsule to a recently discovered planet. Preliminary findings suggest it may be inhabited."

Stearns rolled his eyes upward and breathed a silent prayer.

Kramer straightened, briefcase in hand.

"Wait a minute." Kramer set his coffee on the monitor table and picked up the disk. "Where did this come from?"

Stearns forced a nervous shrug.

Kramer looked the disk over for a label. "Hmm, could I have dropped this?" Finding no markings, he tucked it into his coat pocket, picked up his coffee and started for the door.

Stearns clutched his heart, gasping for breath.

***

Near daybreak the launch countdown began. "Thirteen seconds and counting,"

The controllers watched their monitors with calm indifference knowing the launch would be as successful as the thousands before it.

A voice carried over the loud speakers throughout the facility, "ten, nine, eight."

It was just another probe. It carried no bonus and had no effect on salary or benefits.

"Seven, six, five, four."

Even the local prairie dogs perching atop their mounds outside the compound, watched without fear. The rocket with all its rage and fury would do them no harm.

"Three, two, one, liftoff!"

Flames burst under the rocket and it surged upward gaining momentum.

"One thousand feet per second," came the voice.

The rocket grew smaller as it climbed.

"Approaching mach one."

A sonic boom shook the air, causing the windows in the facility to vibrate, while drawing little attention from the employees within.

As the rocket disappeared from ground view, a second controller announced, "switching to aerial camera."

On the monitors the rocket appeared as a fiery projectile escaping the lens repeatedly only to be recaptured. Finally growing too small and fast for the aerial camera to follow, the rocket disappeared from view.

"Approaching escape velocity," the second controller announced, then added, "we have escape."

An animated simulation on the monitors showed the rocket speeding through space with the earth growing smaller in the background.

"First stage complete. Beginning second stage." The animation showed the rocket separating and the second stage racing forward. "Prepare to disengage nose cone on my mark. Mark!"

The nose cone split apart and a streamlined capsule emerged.

"Roger. Nose cone disengaged. Capsule deployed." A second voice confirmed, "She's on her own. The launch appears to be a success."

The controllers gave each other the casual thumbs up with untailored expressions and returned to their everyday work of plotting the next mission.

From that moment the probe was all but forgotten. It was just another small step for man, another successful launch on the logbooks, another example of tax and spend wrongfully attributed to the interest of science.

*

The capsule raced through space towards an unknown planet, green, and ominous. It penetrated the atmosphere and plummeted ground ward through thick clouds. A chute deployed slowing the capsule's descent.

The planet's inhabitants, hominids, dwarf green and naked, cast their attention skyward, as the capsule swayed gracefully to the planet's surface. Without caution the little green aliens formed a circle around the capsule and watched with astonishment as a video screen opened displaying a western movie. The setting was a saloon crowded with gunslingers, gamblers, and barmaids. The audio was low, but the sound of a player piano playing Buffalo Gals, could be heard over the raucous crowd. A separate, but feminine voice began to resonate from the capsule over the sound of the movie, "We are a peaceful race, a pioneering people."

On screen the scene focused on five cowboys seated at a round table playing poker.

The aliens pressed close to the screen, pointing out everything from cowboy hats and costumes to playing cards and tables. They clenched their chins and scratched their heads with grunts showing their deep interest.

The woman's voice continued, "We have sought to better ourselves by reaching out to our neighbors."

One of the cowboys onscreen drew a gun and pointed it across the table at an unarmed cowboy. The unarmed man stood to his feet and reached out, pleading for his life, while the feminine voice announced, "This outreach has sometimes led to conflict."

The gunman fired across the table killing the unarmed man. The music stopped, and every eye turned to the gunman, as he held the crowd at bay with his pistol, and backed slowly through the swinging doors.

Leaping atop his waiting horse, he rode away at a dead run down the dirt streets.

Within moments a posse formed and rode after the shooter.

Fascinated by the savagery, the little green people differed in reaction from wide eyed astonishment to pointing their fingers as though they were guns and uttering shooting sounds.

Again came the woman's voice, "Yet for the most part we have learned to resolve our conflicts amicably…"

"Amicably?" The aliens looked at one another and repeated the word, tossing it back and forth.

On screen, the posse prepared to lynch the captured gunman from a tree, drawing a chorus of, "Oos and awes," from the planet's inhabitants.

(Year: 2039, same planet)

"Gotta' get away!" Hiroshi's words were mindless and frantic, blurted between labored breaths. He had experienced tough times growing up in the suburbs of Los Angeles, but nothing could have prepared him for this. Swaying floodlights scoured the landscape behind him. The sound of a bugle grew louder, as the posse closed in like baying hounds on the heels of a fox. The thunderous noise produced by the onslaught of robotic horses and the hammering of a hundred steel hooves was rivaled only by Hiroshi's own heartbeat pounding in his ears.

He stumbled through the darkness summoning all the strength he could muster. He wasn't sure why he'd landed on this godforsaken planet, and if he could escape he would never make this mistake again. When he thought he could go no farther the approaching lights revealed the silhouetted form of his spacecraft. He had a chance! Strengthened by the sight, he sprinted on pure adrenaline.

Hiroshi reached the main hatch, fully illuminated by the searchlights glowing from the horse's eyes. With trembling fingers he entered the combination and waited for the hatch to open.

"Stop in the name of the law!" the alien sheriff, dwarf and green, shouted as he skidded his robotic steed to a standstill. He signaled for the posse to circle up. "Stop I say!" The silver badge on his leather vest glimmered despite the ever growing dust cloud which encompassed the band. They coughed as they drew their side-arms and prepared to fire.

Stopping was not an option. Hiroshi flung himself through the opening and pressed "Close," as a barrage of gunfire ricocheted from the door and outer hull. He staggered down the passageway to the cockpit, trying to catch his breath, running his hands along the cold bulkheads to convince himself they were real, and that he had truly escaped. *The ship was impregnable to small arms fire. They could not hurt him now.*

From the cockpit he activated the pre-flight control and auto takeoff system. The sound of the engines rose from a mild hum to a deafening roar, half-drowning the clatter of bullets. Hiroshi semi-collapsed into the pilot seat, mumbling, "Momma told you, but no you wouldn't listen to the old bat."

He clasped the stick with two quivering hands, one to steady the other. The craft responded rising skyward.

***

The posse of small green cowboys watched in disgust as the ship ascended leaving them holding their hats in a storm

10

of wind and dust. One of the deputies took a lariat from the saddle of his robotic horse. Swinging it over his head he released the lasso which fastened to a leg of the craft. The deputy held fast to the lariat as it lifted him from his saddle carrying him upward until he disappeared with the ship in the night sky. Moments later a ten gallon white hat tumbled to the ground landing in the midst of the posse. The frustrated band leaned on saddle horns and stared.

The sheriff broke the silence. "Now what do you suppose Elward is gonna' do without that hat?"

Chapter One
(A stadium in Los Angeles, 2041)

"Veronica, it's time," a voice reminded following a knock on the dressing room door.

"Okay, be out in a minute." She checked her profile in the full length mirror beside an oak vanity. She sucked in her tummy, holding it briefly and releasing it with a dissatisfied sigh. She practiced a few facial expressions; a smile, a wink, a look of erotic pleasure, and a goofy cross-eyed face.

She exited the dressing room at a brisk pace carrying her chin at the "I'm in control" level, while an entourage of makeup personnel met her to install her headset and check everything from her hairpiece to her open-toed sandals with stiletto heels.

Her tight florescent sports bra and form fitting—low cut, white florescent bell bottoms were just a couple of the fashions she had brought back from a bygone era to become trademarks of the Veronica Collection.

Bo, tall, burly and unshaven, wearing the finest Versace sport jacket and pants, looked her over and offered a sarcastic British, "you'll knock 'em dead honey." He turned and strode towards the stage to face the anxious crowd of 80,000, all chanting for Veronica.

The spotlight caught Bo on center stage and silhouetted Veronica's dance team standing motionless in the background.

Bo waited for the noise to die before announcing, "Ladies and gentlemen. Veronicaheads, Please welcome...VERONICA."

The greeting was thunderous but quickly gave way to an even louder pop-techno-rap beat that filled the auditorium. Bo exited the stage with an air of self-importance as the crowd acknowledged their recognition of a song from

Veronica's first cut. The applause rose again as the spotlight found Veronica in the center of her dance team performing a rapid rhythmic choreography in unison with three female and three male dancers all wearing a uniform similar to Veronica's.

Veronica forced a smile and began to sing in the mild raspy style that had carried her to fame almost overnight.

> "Baby baby - I want to feel ya close to me.
> Ya got the moves that I just can't resist..."

Drawing words from memory-turned-habit, Veronica noticed the teenage girls below the stage reciting every word, and imitating every movement with greater enthusiasm than her own.

They eat whatever I feed them, she told herself, without missing so much as a movement or nod.

After three songs Veronica excused the dancers. She took a guitar, a stool and white cowboy hat from behind a speaker and brought them to center stage. She pulled herself atop the stool and positioned the guitar on her lap.

***

"What the hell is she doing?" Bo growled as he leaned forward. "I have half a notion to pull her stupid ass off stage!"

A stage hand standing at Bo's right, shrugged and gulped slightly. "She is Veronica you know. She can do whatever she wants!"

A rock-hard backhand caught the stage hand landing him on the floor beneath Bo's merciless gaze. "Nobody mouths off to me. Now pack up your stuff and get the hell out of here. If I ever see your face again I'll kill ya!"

Bo returned his attention to the stage as the man crawled away on knees and one hand clasping his broken bleeding nose with the other.

"I'd like to do something tonight I've never done before." Veronica placed the cowboy hat on her head, tilting it slightly over her left eye. "I'd like to sing a song I've written which I think you'll enjoy. It's called, 'What's Your Problem, Cowboy?'"

She cleared her throat and strummed once to make sure the guitar was in tune. After a short acoustic intro she sang with a soft voice.

"What's your problem cowboy?
You're long in the saddle and long in the tooth…"

Uninhibited, Veronica played on. The melody seemed to have a spell-binding effect on the crowd with words that could not only be heard, but understood.

As Veronica closed the song, silence fell over the auditorium. Then the first applause inspired a spontaneous and grateful uproar, confirming her assumption, *they ate whatever she fed them.*

She stood and bowed graciously until the lights dimmed. Straightening, she handed the stool, hat and guitar to a stage hand and motioned to the dancers who formed behind her on center stage for the next song.

For the remainder of the show Veronica danced and sang with renewed enthusiasm, inspired by the acceptance she had received from her audience, and for having broken free from the mold in which she felt trapped. After the final bow, she returned to her dressing room. As she entered she discovered Bo waiting inside.

"What do you think you're doing in here?" she demanded with forced vehemence.

"No!" he shouted, shaking a threatening forefinger, as he moved forward, his face brazen, his voice quivering, "The question is, what do you think you're doing? Nobody changes my program!" He grabbed her shoulders with two powerful hands and forced her back against the door. "You sang a redneck song on my stage. In case you've forgotten honey, I own you. I invented Veronica! You're under contract to do as I say." His right eyebrow raised, revealing more of the insanity that already filled his eyes. "And I would destroy anyone who says otherwise! You're mine and don't you ever forget it!" With a final shove he released her. He straightened his sport jacket, popped his neck by tilting his head to one side, then the other, and left the dressing room, slamming the door behind him.

Veronica sat down in the loud ringing silence and sobbed with her face in her hands. Rising to her feet, she summoned the courage she could not find when Bo was present. "I'll show you who owns Veronica," she screamed. Turning to the door, she kicked repeatedly until pain filled her toes. She limped back to her vanity stool where she sat and held her throbbing foot. She wanted to cry, but she needed to act. Rising to her feet, she glanced around the room for something she might use as a disguise. A small table cloth from the vanity top became a scarf, and curtains from the window, a shawl.

After gathering her purse and a change of clothes which she stuffed into a duffle bag, she slipped quietly from the dressing room unnoticed by the crew and scores of paparazzi. She walked with forced confidence down the corridor toward one of the main exits. At the end of the corridor a security guard stopped her.

"What is your business backstage? Do you have a backstage pass?"

Partially concealing her face with the curtain, she said, "Oh, I'm sorry. Is this backstage?" She released a childish giggle, "I was looking for the restroom." Without looking back, she quickly made her way through the stadium into the exiting crowd.

"Whoa dude, whatdja think of the hillbilly song?" someone blurted in a masculine voice.

Keeping her face concealed as she moved forward, Veronica listened and watched as two tall young men conversed. She was taken aback by the first young man's orange perm hairdo, and large nose ring, with matching earrings. *That style went out years ago.*

"Way nostalgical dude!" The second had a white painted face with studded tongue and shoulder length green hair. "And raunchy as hell! Made me wanna garf green slime all over the dude in front of me," he added, pointing his right index finger down his throat.

"Yeah, wa-ay nostalgical and raunchy as hell!" the first agreed, "So give me some tits dude!"

The two young men faced each other and jumped simultaneously, colliding three times at chest level, before landing back to back in a squat, each forcing out a fart.

Veronica gulped and tucked her head in disgust. She considered it ironic that *she should feel so out of place among her own fans.* She grimaced and searched her mind for a pleasant topic to block out the two young men but it didn't seem to help.

"Dude, you better check your undies!"

"No, you better check yours!"

The words, "dude, we'll check 'em together!" were followed by several screams from young women, and then, "gross dude, seriptimoniously gross!"

Veronica turned and pressed into the crowd. She released a sigh of disgust mingled with relief. *At least she was not the center of attention, not at the moment anyway.* She pulled the shawl higher on her face. *She would pretend it was the latest in berca fashioning. After all, stylishness was more about attitude than appearance and shameless self confidence could sell anything. The duffle bag added a nice touch too. Might even start a new fad. The in-vogue Muslim look.*

Near the parking lot the crowd moved faster.

An obese blond woman with flower tattoos on her arms and neck boasted in a loud, but nonchalant voice, "Veronica and I are first cousins. She calls me all the time." The woman held two fingers close together. "We grew up like that."

Veronica rolled her eyes and shook her head. She wanted to call the obese woman a liar, but she feared she would be recognized.

"Shut up an' slap me," a younger girl with pink sunglasses and spiked purple hair, beamed, "Could I have her phone number?"

"No, I'm sorry. I'm not allowed to give it out."

"I'll give you a hundred dollars for it." The younger girl fumbled frantically through her denim jack-o-lantern purse.

"Get real honey, this is 2041, and a hundred bucks won't buy ketchup for my french-fries!"

"I'll give you two hundred," another girl said, holding up the money.

"Well, if it means that much to you." The obese woman took the money and tucked it into her cleavage. She pulled a pen from a purse that seemed minute in contrast to her bare hulking shoulder from which it hung.

"Here, just write it on my arm." The second girl pulled up her sleeve and stared upward, a look of bliss in her eyes. "I'll never wash it off."

Once again Veronica tucked her head and pushed her way through the mob. Outside the stadium the crowd scattered, giving Veronica room to breathe.

As she crossed the parking lot, she noticed two young men leaning on a battered old Buick with a For Sale sign in the back window.

"How much for the car?" she asked.

"A thousand dollars," one of the men replied.

"Got the title?" She dropped the curtain slightly.

The young man squinted, "Haven't I seen you somewhere before?"

Her impulse was *in your dreams, punk!* "Uh-uh, probably at Starbuck's," she blurted, repositioning the curtain to hide the right side of her face.

"Oh yeah, that must be it. On the other hand, must 'a been two other people, never go there." The man looked at his friend. Both smiled.

"I got the title right here, already signed." He reached for his wallet.

Two girls walked by, smiling and laughing, "And I'm like, wow, how many phone numbers have eleven digits?"

The second girl's face grew suddenly pale. Her smile vanished, and her eyes enlarged, as she looked at the phone number on her arm, then at her friend. "Ya think that fat bitch took me?"

Veronica repositioned the shawl to the left of her face. She reached into her purse. "Here's a thousand. Give me the keys."

"How are we supposed to get back to the pad?" The young man looked at Veronica, then at his friend.

"Here's another hundred. Catch one of them yellow checkered things!" She took another bill from her purse, wadded, and threw it over the top of the car, adding, "if there's anything you want in this car get it out now. Oops, too late, honey." She opened the driver's door, tossed the duffle bag onto the thread-bare seat and climbed in. Suddenly she realized she had only what was in her purse. Bo controlled her accounts and without his approval she would soon be broke.

One of the young men opened the passenger door and handed the title to Veronica along with the keys. "Clutch is touchy." He squinted and cocked his head. His eyes widened with surprise. "Wait a minute, you're Veronica!"

"Watch out, I gotta' blow!" She started the car and released the clutch, barely giving the young man time to withdraw before squealing tires and exhaust smoke emphasized her warning.

***

18

"Damn this Rain! Damn this road, and damn this piece-a-shit, ride!" Veronica pulled herself close to the wheel and squinted at the hazy narrow pavement. She could barely hear herself talk, let alone think above the late afternoon down poor which played upon the hood and roof of the old car. The outer windshield had become smattered with road grease from semi-haulers, and the inside was continually fogging. She wiped away the condensation with her hand and cursed the lack of results. If this were a newer car she could switch to Auto Drive, which would activate electronic sensors to guide it, but this car was a relic built long before Detroit had truly modernized. The radio worked from time to time, but Veronica had become exasperated hearing her own songs played repeatedly, and turned it off.

She'd taken a wrong turn from I-5. At least it seemed like a wrong turn now that she was lost on Southern Oregon's back roads in a place called Wimer. She was looking for a hotel, but she found only roads meandering around open pastureland and spotty forests.

Keeping her left hand on the wheel, she opened the glove box and felt for a road map. She found only a molding apple core. Shuddering, she tossed it on the floor and examined the slimy residue on her hand. As her eyes returned to the road, panic gripped her, she hit the brakes and swerved to avoid what appeared to be a large lumbering beast. The car went out of control and skidded across the opposite lane. Veronica closed her eyes. She could feel herself being thrown against the steering wheel, then against the driver's door, as the car came to rest on its side in the ditch.

She lay stunned with her left shoulder against the door until water from the ditch began to soak through her clothes. "Somebody is going to pay!" she shouted as she unfastened her seatbelt. She struggled upright, bracing against a steering wheel that turned almost freely. After rolling the passenger window down, she stepped onto the console and peered across the road oblivious to the pouring rain. She felt her hair bristle. *A man, leading a large brown and white cow along the roadside, had paused for a moment—he and the beast were both staring at her!* She sized the man up quickly. *He wore simple clothes; denim pants, tennis shoes, and a red flannel shirt, therefore he couldn't be very sophisticated. His hair was short, wet, and light brown. He was about six foot with a slim but sturdy appearance, therefore he must be a blue collar type, too stupid for mental work! He had a clean shaven, honest look about him, perhaps even handsome, perhaps very handsome, which meant he was no fun! Finally, he was strolling his cow in the pouring rain, therefore he was a MORON!*

***

Hick tugged gently on the lead rope connecting Bubba's nose ring. He was suppressing a strong urge to give it a good jerk. After all, it was a half-mile home in pouring rain along a narrow road shoulder, and this was the third time in as many weeks the bull had gone looking for greener pastures.

Hog wire and electric fence were not enough to hold a twenty five hundred pound bull, especially when heated heifers bellowed to him like sirens from neighboring pastures.

Hick blamed Bubba's Brahman sire for his roving nature, *although the Hereford on his mother's side certainly contributed.*

"Mix a little ear in your cattle," the old timers had suggested. "Brahman are immune to disease and they're smarter than the average bovine!" Hick rolled his eyes, shook his head and sighed. It was the "smart" he could do without. Besides, Brahman finish slower and aren't ready for market until they are two years old, otherwise Hick would have butchered him several years ago. But Bubba had proven himself, producing the finest crop of bull calves around, and Hick considered him a friend in a way.

"That's the darndest thing I ever saw. That ain't a bull, that's a pussy cat," Old Swede, the neighbor had joked, after watching Bubba scarf down a chocolate candy bar and nudge Hick for more. "If ya ever want to sell him let me know."

But Old Swede wasn't present when Hick tried to ride Bubba or he might have changed his mind.

Mounting the bull from the corral fence, Hick had clung to Bubba's massive hump, but an instantaneous kick and roll ended the ride, and Hick decided not to try again. The decision was not made because of fear since Hick had determined not to be influenced by such emotions. He had learned in his youth to identify fear and suppress it. He had also learned wrestling, boxing, jujitsu, and kickboxing. His prowess had won him the National Championship in ultimate fighting, and given him enough money to buy the ranch.

He could have gone to the international level, but at age twenty nine he realized pride was a greater enemy than fear, and he no longer needed to prove himself. Besides, he liked hurting others less than he liked being hurt. It filled him with sadness seeing a defeated opponent bleeding on the canvass or carried out on a stretcher. Hick's real name was William Hill. As a child he was known as "Billy Hill," which became "Hill Billy," and eventually "Hick."

***

The driveway to the ranch house was in sight when the silence was broken by the sound of skidding tires. An old Buick careened around the corner, sliding from the road, and coming to rest on its side in the ditch across from Hick and Bubba.

At first the car seemed surreal, like a hallucination. The upturned chassis was gray from road dirt and undercoating, holsteined black in spots from oil leaks. It was an unusual sight for Hick since such cars were relics and rarely seen from the bottom. The wheels continued to turn and the motor revved until a solid clunk stopped it. A girl emerged, standing straight up through the passenger window. She glared at Hick, her long blond hair losing body, and

21

darkening with every raindrop, her green eyes alive with anger.

Hick judged her to be in her early twenties. "Pretty," he mumbled, "but too much makeup." Then he called out, "Are you alright?"

She hesitated for a moment, drawing a deep angry breath. "No thanks to you and that beast, you moron!"

Hick forced a smile and signaled adieu with his left hand. "That's all I need to know." *Ingrate! If she was halfway sociable he would have helped her.*

With a gentle tug, he and Bubba resumed their walk.

The girl climbed from the window and jumped to the road shoulder, she moved aggressively towards Hick, her hands swinging violently as she walked. "I wanna know who's gonna' to pay for my car."

Startled by the outburst, Bubba began to bolt, but Hick clutched the bull's head, and gently stroked his neck, calming him.

When the girl had come to a complete stop, Hick met her with a threatening glare and growled, "lighten up lady, or I'll feed you to him for supper!"

Her expression went from anger to astonishment. "Omigosh! Cows are carnivorous? No. I'm almost certain cows eat green stuff, like vegetation, hello!" She rolled her eyes to one side as if to search her memory.

Hick gulped back a smile, *she must be joking, but even so she was cute, cute—like she needs the shit slapped out-a-her, cute!* "Oh yes!" He lowered one eyebrow and took a slow deliberate step toward her. "Definitely carnivorous! Just ask the British. They feed 'em bone meal over there." He watched her complexion turn from red to white. She swallowed gently. Hick raised a solemn right index finger and whispered, shaking it with every syllable, as he leaned toward her, "They only eat grass 'cause there ain't enough meat around to keep 'em satisfied!"

Once again she swallowed. "And I did a milk commercial. I can't believe I did a milk commercial, and actually drank the milk! Uh!" She curled back her lips and clasp her chest.

Hick turned away quickly, knowing he would laugh and feed that *out-a- control ego* if he hesitated. "Come on Bubba. We got no time for theatrics."

Veronica followed cautiously, keeping a safe distance from the bull. "Is there a hotel nearby, or some place I can stay for a couple of days?"

"There is the old Hammel house for rent on West Evans, but it's not furnished. Aside from that, the nearest hotel is twenty miles."

"I just need a place to crash and change my clothes. Is there a boutique near here? I don't even have a dry change of clothes."

Hick stopped and faced her. "Where are you from?"

"I kick around a lot. Not from any particular place." Her eyelids dropped slightly. "Ever hear of California, or is that too cosmopolitan for you?" she said.

He half-turned angrily, "Is twenty-something the new teenybopper, and I don't mean early twenties, or did you never grow up?"

"I've got more important things to do than put up with your insults," she asserted.

Hick shook his head, and turned away. "That sounded like a phrase that you've heard so often, you simply repeat it. And I've got better things to do than stand here in the rain and argue with you." Hick pretended to smile. "C'mon Bubba." He wished the bull could walk faster. "You can stay at my place IF you don't have a place to go," he heard himself say, wondering at the same time where it came from, and clenching his teeth, hoping she'd say no. On the other hand, he couldn't leave anyone stranded in the rain at night and not offer asylum.

***

Veronica hesitated. *This guy could be a rapist or murderer or both.* She glared at the rain drenched road trying to decide whether to stay and die of exposure or follow Hick and face a horrible, torturous death. *No one would ever find her body in this remote place.* Her eyes enlarged with each new thought. *He was, after-all, strolling a beast in the pouring rain. That was definitely weird. Hmmm, he could even be a slasher or something.*

Hick stopped and turned. "Suit yourself," he whispered, picking up the pace.

"Uh, and what will your wife say?" she called out, raising her hand and index finger like a first grader feeling the urge. *He mustn't think she had ever considered him to be a...*

"Wife?" he called back, not missing a step.

"You know, like, uh-significant other, hello?"

"Don't worry about her," he drew a deep breath. "I haven't met her yet."

"Oh!" she feigned relief, as she strode, with hidden reluctance to catch up. "And to think I was worried about what your non-existing wife might say."

***

The light gray athletic sweats were a poor fit, but they were warm and dry, and according to "Roni," as she preferred, "very comfortable." She took interest in his fighting trophies, blowing the dust from each before reading the inscription.

The hardwood floor and solid rock fireplace she described as, "wonderfully archaic."

He would have to look that up although he agreed with her, "completely!"

She was certain there were ordinances prohibiting the wood fire, but when he assured her it was perfectly legal, she settled back and watched it with great satisfaction while she ate popcorn and drank hot chocolate.

24

She was extremely knowledgeable on lots of subjects, not nearly as juvenile as Hick had assumed. She spoke of reintroducing the old "step aerobics program." She said it could be very lucrative. Again he pretended to know what she meant, assuming it to be some form of game. He even donned a pair of reading glasses to appear more informed.

She smiled when she looked at him, and he knew the glasses had been a good idea.

"So what is your ambition? It must be more than raising cattle." She leaned forward, looking him in the eye and squinting her interest.

"I'm a retired fighter and although I love raising cattle, as the money runs out I'll have to do something more." He shrugged slightly and forced an emotionless almost-grin. "I've thought about growing a money crop." He paused, noticing her surprise. "I mean a legal money crop, like Sugar Beats, Echinacea or Jerusalem Artichokes. Maybe I'll just get a job," his voice dropped slightly, "and what about you? What's your ambition?" he asked, caring little about what her reply might be, wanting to shift focus from himself.

A smile crossed her face, she drew a deep breath allowing her eyes to wander across the ceiling. "I want to go to the stars…"

"The stars!' He coughed gently, trying to recover a piece of inhaled popcorn. "I'm sorry, didn't mean to interrupt." He cleared and took a sip of hot chocolate. "Go on, I'm listening."

Roni continued, a serious expression replaced the smile. "They've been colonizing planets for the past twenty years. They even have tourist and passenger transports, and of course there are all kinds of planets: Planets that offer tropical vacations, natural resources, even riches beyond your wildest dreams." Her eyes lit up with excitement.

Hick tried not to show his disinterest. "Yes, but isn't traveling to these places very expensive?"

"Not really, when you consider the present economy and the strength of the dollar, and…" Roni was interrupted by a knock on the door.

"I wonder who that could be." Hick rose slowly from his chair and moved towards the door.

"Wait." Roni pleaded with a sudden gulp. She sprang from her recliner and hurried behind it, whispering, "Let me hide first."

Hick wondered if he should be concerned about a jealous boyfriend or husband. Whatever it was, he would deal with it accordingly. As he opened the door, he caught a glimpse of taillights speeding away. On the porch below him, a puppy, chubby, black with brown mouth, and large brown feet.

"You can come out now," Hick said with dissatisfaction, "Somebody just dumped a dog on me!"

"A dog? You mean like a real canine, kind-a' dog? " Roni stood and rounded the chair with delight and curiosity.

"People around here do that sort of thing. In the summer it's zucchini, and the rest of the year it's dogs and cats." He smiled as he stooped towards the puppy. "You never leave your windows down in a parking lot, people toss bags of zucchini on your seat while you're in the store."

"Oh, let me see it." She forced herself between him and the dog, taking it in her arms and clutching it to her breast in one fluid motion. "My baby boy! I think I'll call you Lucky," she exclaimed in a muffled falsetto, allowing the pup to lick her cheek.

The smile left Hick's face. "Well, it's a girl, and it was dumped on my porch, and I saw it first."

"Your point being?" Roni turned slightly to prevent Hick from seeing the pup. "Then it's Lucki with an I," she said.

"My point being, it's my dog, simple as that!" He nodded and forced a mater-of-fact smile.

"Since I've been here, I haven't seen any cats or zucchini, and no doubt numerous cats and zucchini have been dumped on your door!"

A bewildered expression crossed Hick's face. "What are you trying to say?"

She removed one hand from the dog and shook it at Hick, her expression solemn. "That you feed cats and zucchini, and probably puppy dogs to that beast of yours."

"That's insane!" His jaw dropped, his voice slipped an octave. "I have a cat that lives in the barn. It eats mice."

This time her index finger was accompanied by a confident nod and a low convicting, "So! You feed mice to your cat, and zucchini, and puppies to your cow!"

"What planet are you from?" he almost shouted. "You can't really believe all that!"

"No," she chuckled, "but I really had you going for a minute. And by the way, I am keeping the dog!"

He drew a deep breath, preparing to retaliate. "Oh, what's   the   use!"

Chapter Two

Months passed and Roni became more than a guest. She cleaned Hick's house, clothes, and dishes. Hick thought her language had changed, becoming more down home, more genuine and less hip, although sometimes he wondered if he was the one who had changed or if he just understood her better.

She never mentioned her past, and Hick never asked, he figured she would tell him if she took the notion.

On weekends they dined out or went to movies, and on one occasion, at her insistence, they went night clubbing. Hick was more than a little conscious of his two left feet, but after a few drinks, again at her insistence, he loosened up and began to enjoy himself. Afterward she helped him to the truck and drove home while he slurred old country songs off key, from a slouched position in the passenger seat. She steadied him from the truck to the house and helped him to his bed where they stumbled and fell with her arm trapped under his back.

The following morning Hick awakened with a headache. His recollection of the night before was sketchy although he was certain of he and Roni's romantic involvement. He found her rinsing dishes at the kitchen sink. From the back he caressed her hair gently.

"What do you think you're doing?" she demanded.

He drew back stuttering, "Uh, I thought, I thought you and I were different after last night."

She turned to face him, a look of certainty on her face. "And what did you think happened last night?"

"Well uh…"

"Nothing happened," she asserted, "you got drunk and fell asleep!"

The incident was never revisited. Hitch simply assumed she was telling the truth, and out of embarrassment he decided to distance himself from the incident as much as possible.

***

More than once a stranger in a store or restaraunt remarked how much she looked like Veronica, to which she chuckled. "I get that a lot." When told Veronica had gone missing, and she should apply as her double, she said, "Yeah, but Veronica's like, haaaa (high note), and I'm like, rivet. And besides, I can't dance. I'm dorkier than Hick here." She was certain Hick thought nothing of such talk. He paid less attention to what people thought than he did to changes in Roni's hair and dress, which was slim to none.

She'd made it clear she planned to leave. She spoke with glimmering eyes of the crystalline seas of Kelydar and of shading herself beneath a fruit palm from the warm moons of Montresa. Hick simply listened, seldom commenting, not wanting to discourage her or sound ignorant, he fought the urge to ask, "Where the hell is Kelydar?"

A daily flood of magazines and brochures from travel agencies began to fill the mail box, warning Hick not to expose his true feelings. It was obvious the only thing that kept her on the ranch was Lucki, or Uggy Dog, as Hick called her. (The name had evolved from "Ugly Dog," to "Uggy Dog," as Hick's affection for the animal grew.)

The dog favored Hick, who rose early, taking her on jogs, training her, and playing fetch. She accompanied him on chores, changing sprinklers and feeding cattle. She even rode on the hood of the tractor while Hick plowed in the spring and bailed summer hay, her paws draped over the side in contented bliss. She was an excellent watch dog, keeping visitors and even mail carriers honest and on their guard. She never attacked although those who faced her dared not test her resolve.

29

*

"Breakfast is ready," Roni called. She greeted Hick and Lucki at the door where the morning sun of August cast a line of shade across the porch. Hick noticed her smile lacked its usual luster.

"Is something wrong?" He hesitated on the concrete porch before removing his boots.

"Come inside." She motioned with a nod. "Nothing's really wrong it's just…"

Hick set his boots down and entered, allowing Uggy Dog to follow before closing the door to keep out the late summer bugs. He inhaled the piping aroma of hash browns and eggs, hoping the savor would calm his fear of what she might say.

"I'm leaving," she began, "I bought tickets." Her lips quivered slightly, she swallowed. "I told you from the beginning I was leaving."

"Tickets? Don't you mean a ticket?"

She turned her gaze to the floor. "I bought a ticket for you in case you want to come along. Swede, next door has been trying to buy you out for years." She pointed toward the window. "He's offered a pile of money but you won't sell."

Hick drew a deep breath, holding it briefly before saying, "I can't go, this ranch is my life. I have to stay here. I want to stay here, and I'd like you to stay with me," again he hesitated. The words were hard to say, "and marry me. I never asked before because I knew you'd say no. Now it doesn't matter anyway. I just want you to know how I feel. Because after you leave, you'll still know that I love you."

She pressed her left hand against her forehead and turned away sobbing. "Hick, I've never loved anyone except myself. If I did love someone, it would be you. Truth is I'm not ready to settle down."

He took a difficult breath. "So where did you get enough money to buy these tickets?"

"I drew it from an old bank account. I've had it all along. In fact, I have enough for both of us if you change your mind."

He shook his head and whispered, "When do ya' leave?"

"Today," she said softly, turning back to face him while wiping a runaway tear from her cheek. "I have a cab coming to pick me up this afternoon."

"I'll miss you," he said, following with a sad chuckle, "It will be lonely around here, just me and the dog…"

"Lucki?" her voice raised somewhat in contentious surprise. "I'm taking Lucki with me."

"I hope you don't think I'd give you my dog!" He half-shouted.

"We'll see about that!" She rose from the table.

"Yes we will," he agreed, standing and turning back to the door, "C'mon Uggy Dog," he commanded, holding the door for himself and the dog, and closing it with more than the usual force. He slipped his boots on and stomped toward the barn. "Nobody's gonna' take you away from me," he said, patting the dog's head as she pranced along beside him.

***

"Mr. William Hill!" A masculine British voice called from the floor of the barn.

Hick turned from the loft, where he was stacking hay bales, to see a large burly man in a black suit and tie, with black chauffeur's hat and gloves.

Uggy dog lunged from the loft with a terrorizing howl and started down the bales toward the man, but a solid, "get back here," from Hick, stopped her, and she waited for him to descend.

Hick looped a piece of bailing twine and tied the dog to an upright beam. "Stay," he commanded, as he approached the man. "What can I do for you?"

Uggy dog continued to growl softly as though she knew better than to defy Hick.

31

"I have a problem. Maybe you can help me solve it." The man drew a snub nosed .38 revolver from his coat pocket and pointed it at Hick's face. "You see, you have something of mine, and I've come to get it back!"

"What would that be?" Hick showed little emotion, watching the man's every move for the slightest mistake.

"Veronica!" The man stated with moderate intensity as though Hick should know.

"You mean," Hick hesitated, "Roni?"

"Turn around," the man ordered in a smug but make-no-mistake voice.

Hick turned slowly.

***

Roni strode toward the barn, wiping half-dried tears and donning a much happier expression. She'd made up her mind, she would stay and marry Hick. It had become crystal clear to her. She loved Hick. She had found contentment with him and she would let him know. She carried in one hand the tickets to her former dreams which she would give up for him. She practiced her acceptance speech, "Yes! I will become Mrs. William Hill," but something was wrong. Lucki was barking. Roni added spring to her stride, hurrying through the large double doors into the barn's semi darkness. "What is it, Lucki?" she half shouted.

As her eyes adjusted she was able to answer her own question. Hick was lying face down on the barn floor, with Bo standing over him, pointing a gun at Hick's head. "No! Please, Bo," she screamed. I'll do anything! Anything!"

"Really? Anything? Bo un-cocked the revolver and stepped towards her. Placing his gun hand around her neck, he pulled her close and brushed her cheek with an emotionless kiss. "And what have we here?" He took her by the wrist and raised her ticket hand to eye level. "Hmm, two tickets to paradise, just for you, and me, and a dog." Again he kissed her cheek, drying her tears with his rough face. "There

there, don't cry. You and I will go on the dream vacation of our lives."

"Is he alive?" she shuddered, more angry than frightened.

"Of course, darlin', he just had a little collision with my gun. He'll be just fine when he awakens."

"How'd you find me?"

"You made a little withdrawal from an account, but you forgot that I have friends in opportune places, like your bank, and your travel agency. As a matter of fact when your travel agent informed me of your plans, I booked publicity tours on six planets. So get packed and do as I say, and I won't hurt your boyfriend or your dog anymore."

***

Hick tried to pull himself to a sitting position, but the slightest movement made him nauseous. He settled back and watched the moon through the cracks in the barn wall. By now Roni was long gone on her way to that dream planet with her violent boyfriend. *They deserved each other.* Even the thought sent a sharp pain shooting through his head. Hick turned towards the loft where Uggy Dog had been tied. She was gone. Tears formed in his eyes. Not only had Roni made a mockery of his love, she had taken his companion.

Hick struggled to his feet and staggered to the barn door where dizziness overtook him. To keep from falling, he lowered himself to the ground where he retched violently. An hour passed before he tried again, making it all the way to the front porch. Another hour passed before he reached his bed where he remained until mid afternoon the following day.

He did very little during the week. By Friday night of the second week his body had recovered, but a deeper pain filled his heart. *Drinking helps one forget, or so he had been told.* He knew of a bar where they held *tough guy* competition, a form of ultimate fighting. ***The Rodeo!*** He had even been invited there from time to time to fight amateurs, but fighting to entertain a crowd of drunks seemed pointless. Now he would like nothing more than to get drunk and knock some heads. He fired up his old cattle truck and drove to The Rodeo.

The parking lot was filled with relic trucks like his own. The only exceptions being an occasional Porsche, parked cockeyed to prevent body damage. Hick could hear loud country music along with shouts and cheers coming from within. "What the heck?" he muttered, as he neared the entrance, noticing the large neon sign above the building had been changed from "**The Rodeo**" to "**The Virtual Rodeo**." Two cowgirls were helping a cowboy, one under each arm, as he hobbled from the bar with a heavily bandaged ankle. Their laughter seemed ironic to Hick considering the man's injury, yet it spoke of hope for his wounded heart.

Hick waited at the door for a stretcher to be carried out. "Don't let 'em get ya on Herman," the injured man's advice was almost drowned by cheers and shouts from within.

A man with a metal money box addressed Hick from behind a portable card table just inside the door, "that'll be forty bucks sir, includes your virtual goggles and one ride. The prize is five hundred dollars if you can ride the bull for eight seconds, and a date with Charlotte, the rodeo queen."

Hick fumbled through his pockets, producing forty dollars in wadded bills. In return he received a red ticket labeled, "One Ride," along with a pair of damaged, possibly bloodstained virtual goggles.

The ball room was large with an elevated bar at one end and tall bar stools surrounding the perimeter, a cowboy or cowgirl on each. Smoke filled the air, and sawdust was scattered on the floor here and there. In the center of the room a series of tracks criss-crossed one another. Positioned between the stools on the far side of the room was a mechanical bull.

Hick placed the goggles over his eyes and the room became a rodeo arena. The patrons on stools appeared to be seated on a board fence. The mechanical bull was in a chute. His lines and horns were Limousine, seemingly authentic except for the steam billowing from his nostrils. The bar remained unchanged although it was elevated above and behind a board fence.

Hick slipped through an opening in the fence and up a staircase to the bar where he motioned for the bartender.

The bartender approached. "What'll it be? Say, do I know you? You're not that Hill kid, "Hick," who won the national title?"

Hick took a step back from the bar. "Well, uh."

"Even with them virtual goggles, and that beard, I'd know you anywhere." The bartender pointed at Hick's face. "Hey guys, this here is Hick Hill, the national ultimate fighting champion!"

Hick raised his hands, palms out, trying to play down the bartender's introduction, as the cowboys at the bar crowded in to shake his hand.

"Somebody buy him a drink before I do it myself. Whataya havin' Hick?"

"Surprise me but make it strong," he shouted, shaking one hand after another, each cowboy reminding him to ride Herman and offering to buy him the next drink.

"I wouldn't want to disappoint anyone," Hick said, as the bartender handed him the first drink. He guzzled it quickly, shuddering and grunting as it went down. The men around him cheered and called to the bartender for more.

"You may as well just leave the bottle," Hick added.

"Ah just keep linin' 'em up there, barkeep," one cowboy corrected, smiling at his friends and nodding towards the bull. "I'll bet we got us a champion cowboy here." He glanced at Hick's shoes, adding, "in sneakers and slacks. What a trendsetter!"

"Hey, cowpoke." Hick nodded when he had the man's attention. "I left the cows at home. I come out here to have fun, and I don't need no boots and hat to make people think I'm somethin' that I'm not." Hick motioned to the man's clothes.

The man faced Hick, towering over him and glaring down in a condescending manner.

"Don't even think about it," Hick warned.

"I wouldn't if I were you, Jake," said the bartender.

Jake scoffed, turned and walked away.

Hick had several one-mores until his eyes fixed on a woman five stools away. She looked like Roni despite her white cowboy hat, vest and white denim jeans. "Whoa. No more whiskey." He raised his hands in surrender, then he pointed down the bar, "Can somebody tell me who that is?"

"Well, that there's Charlotte the rodeo queen. You can win a date with her if you can ride Herman for eight seconds," one of the cowboys offered, laughing as though he had heard a great joke. "And ya get a big kiss after the ride."

"She looks like Roni," Hick slurred.

"Yeah, she's a virtual mockup of your dream girl, whoever you want her to be." Again the cowboy laughed.

"I'd ride ten bulls for her." Hick sprang to his feet. "Bring on the bull."

"Bartender," one cowboy shouted. Turning back to Hick he added, "Give your ticket to the bartender." He motioned across the bar, his voice dropped slightly as though in sadness, perhaps excitement, Hick couldn't tell.

The bartender moved down the bar accepting Hick's ticket. "Are ya' sure ya' want to do this, Hick?"

"Heck yeah, bring on the bull. I'm gonna break that sucker to ride."

Hick bellowed a "Yeeehaa," as he started across the arena to the chute where the bull appeared to be trapped. A group of long neck bottle toting cowboys followed hooting and hollering.

Hick hurled himself over the board fence and onto the bull's back.

Raising a victorious fist, he shouted, "Yeeehaa, cut this sucker loose."

One of the cowboys instructed him to grip a rope on the bull's shoulder with his left hand, keeping his right hand free. "If ya' make it past eight seconds, ya' win the prize."

"Sounds simple enough, what are we waiting for. Let 'er go."

"Okay, hang on."

The bull bolted from the chute, bucking, kicking and spinning. It moved forward at a high speed, then slowed, turned, whirled and kicked. Hick held on trying to anticipate the bull's movement, leaning, and countering every jerk, jolt and yank. "Is that all you got? Is that all you got?" he screamed, stopping only when he realized he was laying on his back looking at the steel truss overhead. As the cheers and laughter died, Hick couldn't help but notice the song, What's Your Problem, Cowboy? carried over the speakers.

"Are you alright, sugar?" a coarse, less than feminine, southern voice whispered. She leaned and kissed him gently. It was Roni. Something wasn't right. Her upper lip felt bristly, and her breath carried an unsavory odor, but for Roni he would endure anything.

"I love you Roni, please come back, live with me and be my wife," he blurted.

"Why sure, sugar," she responded. "Boys, take him to my room."

***

The room was dark, the air reeked of pungent perfume mingled with the odor of scented candles. A hard coil spring mattress creaked beneath him at the slightest movement. Hick could hear the muffled sound of a shower and a coarse, low, voice singing off key, from another room. It was that song, "What's Your Problem Cowboy?"

The stretcher ride to the cottage behind the bar seemed like a distant dream. Hick peered about in the darkness trying to piece together all the events of the evening. He could recall the sound of the door opening and closing, as he was carried into the cottage, and the feeling of being dumped from the stretcher onto the bed. Some things remained vague or escaped him completely. His shirt was missing, and he didn't know why, "Roni, where are you?" he called.

"I'm coming, sugar," the raspy voice replied.

"He heard footsteps thumping hard against the floor. The bed swayed and tilted, as she climbed next to him. He felt her skin, cold and damp, pressing against his bare chest, her bristly lip on his, her forehead against his goggles.

His goggles? He reached up to remove them.

"By the way, those don't work in here," she growled.

"You're not Roni!" He rolled her to one side and sprang from the bed onto wobbly legs. Staggering back, he braced himself against the wall.

"So, nobody's perfect." She smiled. Her body, nude except for a bikini bottom, half concealed under layers of fat, her skin, pale, oily, obese, and well wrinkled glistened in the light of a dozen candles. She threw back her short red-gray hair with a quick sensuous flick. "I don't know who this Roni is you keep talking about. My name is Charlotte, and you and I are engaged, sugar." She rolled from the bed, her double chin tucked tightly against her neck, her gaze fixed like a laser upon him, she slunk toward him. Every movement spoke of slow, deliberate seduction.

"Not anymore," he shouted, his eyes scouring the room with near hysteria for the exit. He tried to escape, but an oily arm encircled and clutched him with the strength of two men. He struggled but could not break free. Instinctively Hick's knee shot upward catching Charlotte between the legs. She stumbled back. It looked as though she would recover, but he pushed her to the floor and darted past her, diving head first through an open window into the darkness.

***

From a redwood deck behind the bar, a group of ten cowboys sat around patio tables nursing longnecks in the moonlight. Their hats moved slowly in unison following the barefoot, half naked form sprinting across the parking lot. One of them shook his head. "I told you he didn't have what it takes. Now where's that hundred you owe me?"

The bartender drew a hundred dollar bill from his pocket and slapped it in the cowboy's hand. "There's nothing like love to sober a man up, is there boys?"

In   unison   the   cowboy   hats   slowly   nodded.

Chapter Three

The sky was overcast, offering a pleasant break from an otherwise hot summer. A mild wind caressed Hick's bruised face, as he walked down the driveway, a bucket of grain in each hand. The breeze felt good although it would have felt better the day before when he was recovering from a painful hangover. Two dozen Hereford followed anxiously along the inside of the fence anticipating their morning meal. Hick poured the grain over the fence into feed troughs distributing it evenly among the cattle. He thought how happy he had been before Roni came, and how unhappy he was now. *It would have been better had he never met her, but that was bygone water, and he had bridges to cross.*

A late model red Oldsmobile turned into the driveway and rolled to a stop. Recognizing the driver as the bartender from The Virtual Rodeo, Hick rounded the car.

The bartender handed Hick an envelope. "You forgot to pick up your winnings."

Hick shook the envelope gently, feeling the cash slide around inside. "Sorry you had to come all the way out here for this."

"Well, Hick, actually I didn't come all the way out here for that. There's another reason. Charlotte has announced her engagement." He handed Hick a copy of the local newspaper.

Hick recognized his likeness on the front page beside a picture of Charlotte. The caption read, "**Ex-champion fighter to wed**." His heart raced, his jaw dropped, he felt his hands crumple the paper.

The bartender continued, "it's in every paper in the State. Charlotte says she has ten witnesses that heard you propose and ten more that claim you went to bed with her. If you don't marry her she will allege that you proposed in order to have consensual sex, after which you beat her up. She says she feels tricked and dirtied, and she'll file criminal charges for rape and battery along with a civil suit for breach of affection if you don't go through with the wedding. Beings you're the champ and all, your hands are lethal weapons, and remember, her daddy happens to be the District Attorney."

Hick swallowed hard unsure of what to do. *He should have gone with Roni when he had the chance.* "Wait a minute, isn't there some law that says that fugitives of misdemeanors who keep from getting caught for seven years can no longer be charged. Some kind of statute of limitations?"

The bartender thought for a minute. "I think you're referring to that law under the New Homestead Act, where you can homestead one of those planets in the Emma Quadrant. They give ya' immunity from prosecution. It's an effort by the government to maroon suspected criminals where they can do no harm, while reducing the burden on taxpayers for court and prison costs. They encourage fugitives to bring livestock with 'em." He nodded towards the cattle. "Of course it might not be any better than prison."

"Hmmm," Hick nodded, a whirlwind of ideas turned in his mind all culminating on one conclusion. He felt a sinister smile forming on his face. "Tell Charlotte to give me two weeks to recover from my injuries and I'll see her weekend after next."

*

Hick wasted no time planning his escape. Swede, his neighbor, agreed to buy the ranch and most of the cattle with the exception of Bubba and two of his best cows.

After closing bank accounts, Hick notified the telephone and electric companies. He phoned the travel agencies from Roni's brochures, until he found the best deal on travel and destination. He selected a planet much like Oregon with trees and green rolling hills, creeks, rivers, and lakes. He posted "yard sale" signs, labeling everything from furniture to trophies at must-sell prices.

With every heirloom and piece of furniture he relinquished, Hick became more determined to leave. Within two weeks all that remained were three bovine and enough items and equipment to start his new life.

*

Hick arrived at the space facility in his old truck with cattle trailer in tow. He had never believed in destiny, but the rows of waiting spacecraft along the tarmac seemed to beckon to him, *come and fulfill your dreams.*

Guards at the main gate were very hospitable. "Oh yes, Mr. Hill, we've been expecting you. The valet will take your truck and livestock to the staging area where the animals will be loaded on the spacecraft."

The valet stepped forward, smiled and held out his hand for the keys.

"They're waiting for you in the briefing room as we speak." The man guided Hick across the hall into a room where he watched a series of videos in 3D, expounding on every aspect of space travel and the latest technological advances.

Afterward Hick was introduced to his pilot.

"Hiroshi? Did I say that right?" Hick squinted, extending his right hand.

Hiroshi was about 5' 10, thirtyish, with short black hair and an oriental look about him. Hick supposed him to be attractive judging by the way the pretty blonde attendant smiled as she introduced him.

"Yes, 'Hiroshi'!" He shook Hick's hand before casting a quick wink at the attendant. "I'm your pilot, navigator and bombardier."

"Bombardier?" Hick felt his eyes widen.

"It's a private joke." Hiroshi smiled. "I'll tell you more about it during our voyage." Turning, he pointed through a wall of windows onto the tarmac. "That's our ship. She's a freighter. I guess you opted for a freighter because of your cattle. Did they tell you about the advantages and disadvantages of a freighter?"

Hick nodded. "Yeah, they said the main advantage was I could leave sooner. And the disadvantages are three lonely months just you and the pilot."

Hiroshi motioned for Hick to accompany him down the well-waxed marble hallway. "Dude, most people like the passenger cruises because they're looking for a relationship. You know the way they advertise those cruises; handsome dude, delicious babe, dancing the zamba under the Cantalic moons." Hiroshi held his fingers up as quotation marks. "A romance among the stars. But dude, if you're not looking for romance this ship has all the comforts you could ask for."

Hick nodded agreeably although he'd never heard of the Zamba, and knew nothing of the Cantalic moons. "Believe me I'm not looking for romance," he said.

"No, I heard you were running from one." Hiroshi chuckled mildly.

Hick's jaw loosened, a terrible habit for a fighter, one he thought he'd broken years ago. "Word travels fast," he said, trying to look unsurprised.

Hiroshi hid his smirk with his hand. "Ahem." He seemed to be searching for a new topic. "Dude, did they counsel you on cryostasis?"

"I prefer to be awake." Hick's voice and expression were disconcerted. "They said it's not a perfected science."

Hiroshi chuckled. "True, but they are making advances in that technology, and who knows, maybe someday it will be the way to travel, but for now, if it ain't tight, it ain't right. Come on I'll show you the ship."

*

The craft was about a hundred feet long, and almost as wide. It was saucer shaped with front cockpit windows and fins in back. Eight wheels mounted on four struts gave the craft a five foot lift and, according to Hiroshi, the ability to taxi like an aircraft if necessary.

Hiroshi led Hick up a graded aluminum loading ramp which extended from the ground to a sliding hatch door. "Check out the entry panel." He pointed to four rows of numeric keys on the hull beside the hatch. "The combination is 3547 in case you're locked out and need to get in quickly, like moskoshi dude."

Hick felt his lips tighten into a smile. "Locked out?" He released a half-chuckle, but noticing Hiroshi's somber expression, allowed the smile to fade. "3547," he repeated.

Hiroshi continued through the hatch into a passageway. He pointed out the cattle compartment with its restraints for take-off and landing, and a vacuum system with a three inch hose for cleaning. He stopped briefly at the head where he explained the advantages of the newly installed vacuum water closets, how they eliminated the life-threatening danger of airborne waste during takeoff.

He pointed out the berthing compartment. "You can bunk wherever you want, I'm not particular. Over here is the crew lounge. As you can see, the ship is designed for more than two people." Hiroshi stepped inside and nodded for Hick to follow. "That's the entertainment center complete with books, music and movies, surround-sound audio and virtual 3D video. There's a compact multi-gym which offers the finest zero gravity workout." Hero pointed to a hatchway on his right. "To starboard we have a zero grav hot tub and sauna. And back here at the aft bulkhead is a wet bar with packets of reconstitutable soft drinks, beer, wine, champagne and 180 proof alcohol in every flavor. My weakness is sake'."

"I rarely drink." Hick surveyed his surroundings, trying to imagine what life would be like after they got underway. *Oh well,* he told himself, *at least we'll have entertainment,* although he was already beginning to miss home and the way of life he had known for so long.

Meanwhile back at the ranch.

A new red Cadillac turned from the main road, and rolled down the driveway, coming to a stop in front of the ranch house.

An obese woman in a tight formal lavender gown and elbow length white gloves emerged from the front passenger door. She took a drag from a cigarette on a long plastic tip and lowered her sunglasses, scouring the silent premises.

"Doesn't look like there's anyone home, Charlotte," the driver pointed out in a meek hesitant tone.

Charlotte exhaled a cloud of smoke. She drew a deep breath and released a scream of rage that echoed through the canyon to the surrounding hills and back sending livestock scurrying and flocks of birds to flight. "Nobody makes a fool of   Charlotte   McHenries!"

Chapter Four

Hick leaned back in the lounge recliner and stared at the starboard bulkhead chuckling at something Hiroshi had said. The voyage had been long and boring, passing through countless miles of space with more of the same ahead. He'd enjoyed Hiroshi's collection of movies, most of them medieval with a handful of swashbucklers in the mix, but now they just reminded him of Earth and Veronica.

"Little green bastards?" Hick looked mildly amused. "You mean like little green Martians?"

Hiroshi leaned forward, a serious expression on his face. "I mean little green shit-kick'n dudes, masquerading as cowboys. The correct term is Munchipods." He took a swig from a sake' bottle before setting it back on the bar.

Hick shook his head and left the lounge, he'd had all he could take of Hiroshi's nonsense. Hiroshi followed him to the cockpit.

"There she is." Hiroshi pointed through the cockpit window at a large green planet suspended amid the nothingness of space, half-illuminated by the light of a distant sun. The planet had an emerald, candy-like appearance, and seemed much closer than it was. Two moons, pale in contrast, hung in orbit around her with traces of a third moon eclipsed behind.

"We're going in, and it's gonna' be a bumpy ride," Hiroshi said, "so you'll have to restrain the cattle."

"This is not our destination!" Hick leaned forward in his seat. He had a bad feeling about making an unscheduled stop. "I'd like to know something. What business do we have here? Do we need food, water, supplies? What's the deal?"

Hiroshi glared at Hick, his eyes reddened from alcohol. "First off Hick, you contracted an empty freighter on its way to pick up valuable cargo, therefore your fare was cut in half.

You could hardly expect first class. Secondly, we're not stopping on the planet's surface. We're just going to do a little personal business."

"Yes, but it's your own personal business, right?"

"Hick, I'm the captain, so any problem you have has to be taken up with my superiors. Our operating standards allow some deviations for personal reasons, as long as it doesn't encumber the mission, and since I've heard you don't want to return to Earth, you may as well strap in the cattle, lighten up, kick back and enjoy the ride. Just remember one thing, , the little samurai's in charge."

Sub Chapter A

Meetings during happy hour in the Munchville saloon were like meetings of the Areopagus in Athens. Much was said, much consumed but little accomplished.

Munchipods wishing to socialize and address community issues met here, and Clint, a small green nobody, determined to be somebody, was no exception.

Clint slid his chair back from the barroom table and lowered himself to the floor, his cowboy hat alone protruding above the table top. "Excuse me, I got somethin' to say," he shouted, his voice, high pitched, and miniature, overshadowed by the rabble of small green cowboys all vying to be heard.

"Hang 'em high," one cowboy bellowed in an almost vibrato tone.

"No, hang 'em low," another contended, "it's more fun to watch 'em swing when their toes can almost reach the ground."

"I say just shoot 'em," a third shouted, inciting a roar of unanimous disapproval from the crowd.

Clint climbed atop his chair and drew his revolver. He fired twice at the ceiling. A dead silence fell over the saloon as the echo from the shots diminished.

Every tiny green eye turned and fixed on Clint.

"Uh." He looked around the room at his astonished audience unable to remember what he wanted to say. Suppressing the urge to gulp, he gritted his teeth and forced his chest outward. "It seems to me," he began, as he lowered his gun and blew the smoke from the barrel, "Uh, what is it they call us?"

"Munchipods!" a bystander reminded.

"Munchipods eh? Why it seems to me, them humans wouldn't know a real cowboy if he bit 'em in the ass."

"Yeah!" the crowd agreed.

"Why is it they keep landin' here?"

An unarmed cowboy with large wire-rim glasses half-raised his hand and began to speak, "It has something to do with the centrifugal force in our outer stratosphere."

"No, Sodbuster!" Clint reprimanded "It's because they need to see how real cowboys live. Now they think we can't cowboy up, but we could show 'em a thang or three."

"Yeah," the crowd shouted.

Clint pulled a pouch of tobacco and cigarette paper from his double seamed western shirt. "We ought to make slaves out of 'em, and teach 'em not to look down on us." He shook some tobacco into the paper then rolled it. After licking the seam, he twisted the ends and gently placed it between his lips. Cocking his head, and speaking from the corner of his mouth, he said, "who's got a light?" A dozen small green hands extended with lit matches. He leaned forward and touched the cigarette to the nearest match. After drawing a deep breath, he released a cloud of smoke with a cough. "Thanks partner," he said, nodding to no one in particular. "Now, they say the alien woman is a sanger! That means she can sang, so she's not totally worthless." He took a drag and exhaled a large smoke ring. "And the alien man, well he could do manual labor, but the interestinest thing is the aminal that was with 'em. What did they call it?... a Doeg?"

Members of the crowd nodded, repeating the word, "doeg."

Clint stepped one boot onto the table and rested his elbow against his bended knee. He tapped the ashes from the end of his cigarette and watched them fall to the floor. "They say that aminal took old Sour Dough's leg off." Clint snapped his fingers. "One bight!"

The crowd groaned in shock.

Clint cocked his head. "Seems to me an aminal like that could make some money, put on display."

A layer of cowboy hats seemed to rock in unison as the group nodded their approval.

***

Hiroshi grunted against the force of entry "They'll be fine," he said, as if he knew what Hick was thinking, "Those cattle restraints are designed to withstand weights of over one hundred thousand pounds. I haven't lost a cow yet," he added, as the ship angled slightly and the pressure lessened.

From the side window, green continents and oceans increased in size. Mountains seemed to form and the landmass grew larger, flattening into smooth plains that spread like an unwrinkled blanket all the way to the distant horizon.

Hiroshi activated a screen on the dash. A menu appeared from which he selected "Planet M." "This is a global locator. It's like a G.P.S., but it works without satellites. I mapped the coordinates last time I was here." He pointed to a small flashing cursor and a dot labeled, *Munchville*. "We're here, but our target is here. We'll make two passes. On the first pass the sonic blast will bring them out into the streets. On the second pass I'll dump our onboard waste.

Hick smiled helplessly. "You must really hate them."

"Last time I was here they caught me and stuck me in their jail. They were going to auction me off as a slave, but I escaped."

"Sounds pretty intense." Hick's tone seemed lacking in interest.

"Dude, it was grueling!" Hiroshi shook his head as he eased forward on the stick, "hang on we're swoopin' in."

The craft tilted forward, increasing in speed until a mild hum of wind resistance grew and gained an octave.

Easing back, Hiroshi leveled the craft about one hundred feet above the ground. Roads and rooftops flew by beneath the cockpit window.

"You'll get a better view of Munchville on the next pass. It's actually more than a mile in length," Hiroshi said, seemingly in response to the way Hick stretched and turned his neck to catch a glimpse of the alien town. "In fact, I'll pass over it slowly so you can get a good look."

Hiroshi eased the craft around, causing it to slow as it turned, until the outlying countryside, with scattered trees and green rolling hills seemed like a topographical exhibit at a county fair.

"And now for the grand finale." He straightened and leveled the craft as the small town came into view with its dirt streets and shake roofs. "Bombs away," he chuckled pressing a button labeled "waste door." The door made a whirring sound as it opened, and the craft seemed to gain altitude as it lightened.

"Are those munchipods?" Hick pointed at a crowd gathered in the street. "Looks like they're shooting guns into the air!"

A hail of bullets clattered against the hull as the ship passed.

"Don't worry about it. Dude, we're impregnable. They could shoot all day and never bust a tile. In fact…" Hiroshi's words were cut short by a zinging ricochet within the hull, followed by a solid thunk!

"What about the waste door?" Hick's face filled with concern. "If a bullet entered the waste door what damage could it do?"

"It could puncture the fuel tank." Hiroshi leaned forward observing a flashing red light on the dash. "Dude, we've been compromised! We're losing fuel pressure!"

"So, what can we do?" Hick felt the temperature rising in his cheeks and forehead.

Hiroshi's face took on a pale white color. He drew a deep breath. "We'll have to set her down."

"Of all the stupid stunts. I tried to tell you we had no business here, but no, you wouldn't listen. You had to dump shit on the munchipods, just to satisfy your own stupid ego, and now look at us. I want my money back!"

"Dude, deal with the unsuppressed emotions. I have to find a place to set down. It has to be well hidden, and I don't need your input right now."

Hick shook his head in disgust and leaned back in his seat.

"There! At the edge of that cliff behind those high rocks." Hiroshi pointed. "We may be able to hide the ship in there."

Hiroshi brought the ship to a hovering position at the edge of the cliff and lowered it slowly between the cliff face and the outlying rocks onto a sandy surface below. The engines powered down slowly until an uncanny silence filled the air.

"We have two choices." Hiroshi's tone lacked his usual confidence and zeal. "We can radio home for help, which I'd rather not do, or we can go to the munchipods and sweet talk them into helping us. A rescue from Earth is months out, and if we sit here long enough the munchipods will be on us like flies on feces. I'll leave it to you."

"I see." Hick nodded facetiously. "Now that you've got us into this mess, you'll just leave it up to me to get us out. Well I'll go to the munchipods and I'll tell them it was all your idea to drop shit on them. Maybe that'll appease them. Right now I want to get as far away from you and this ship as I can."

***

Hick left the ship and set out towards the small alien town of Munchville. He carried a flask of water and a communicator in case he should need to call for help, although the thought of contacting Hiroshi for any reason repulsed him.

The rocky terrain gave way to green rolling hills and Hick found himself fascinated by the scenery. The feeling of walking on solid ground felt strange, yet it reminded him of Earth. He marveled at the way the sunlight filtered through the green clouds, casting a lime tint on his skin. He thought how happy Bubba would be to see the grass and open plains after months in a small compartment with nothing to eat but dry alfalfa pellets.

Pausing for a moment he drew a deep breath. The air was like fresh roses and love and all the feelings one gets on the first true spring day. In his mind he saw Roni picking daffodils along a country road in the lacy white dress he'd bought her. A smile formed on his lips and a tear in his eye. *Those days were wonderful. Would he ever see times like that again?*

Chapter Five

Hick stood on a hill looking down at the motionless town of Munchville. Simple wood buildings with board walkways spanned both sides of a dirt street. Signs written in English identified the saloon, general store, jail, livery stable, and more. Robotic horses stood like statues at hitching posts, the majority in front of the saloon. The town smelled of cow manure from Hiroshi's bombing run, and wood smoke, which oozed from brick chimneys above the rooftops. The song "Buffalo Gals," hammered on a player piano, accompanied by enthusiastic helium voices came from the saloon. Hick pinched himself hard before starting down the hill.

The music and gaiety grew louder as he passed between buildings and crossed the empty dirt street. He paused briefly at a hitching post to look over one of the robotic horses. It was about fourteen hands, brown with saddle, stirrups, bridal and reins. He reached out to touch the horse's neck, but it turned with a whinny and bit him on the arm.

"Ouch damn it!" Hick whispered, jerking his arm back. The bite stung but failed to break the skin. "I hate horses," he muttered as he turned towards the saloon. He pushed through the swinging doors and entered, ducking slightly to keep from bumping his head on the door frame. The large room was smoky and poorly lighted. Six female dancers performed on stage, kicking and throwing up their cancan dresses with multi layered petticoats. They were barely three foot tall with green skin and hair.

Crystal chandeliers hung overhead, and paintings of dwarf green women dressed as showgirls decorated the walls. An audience of small green cowboys, miners and gamblers, three feet tall, well armed and intoxicated, sat around bar tables singing and cheering. A staircase, broad at the base with an ornate wooden rail tapered upward to a second floor.

The piano struck a flat note and died. The dancers scurried from the stage screaming, and the whoopla gave way to the sound of rustling chairs and tables, as tiny gunslingers sprang to their feet, whirling to face Hick, readied for the draw.

A tense silence followed.

Hick forced a smile and a stiff one-handed wave. "Ahem, hi, I'm William Hill, and you're probably wondering why I'm here. I-I am an ambassador from Earth, that's a far away planet, and I bring you greetings. Would you take me to your leader."

"You ain't no ambassador," a munchipod with a mustache and a turned-up hat stepped forward, shaking a stern finger, "you's one of them runaway slaves."

"No," Hick shook his head, "I've never been a slave, I'm an..." *what was the word he was looking for? Words always escaped him under pressure. "Emissary! I'm an emissary."*

"Then somebody should put you out of your em-misery," blurted one munchipod, taking a half step forward, his fingers twitching slightly above two six-guns.

"Back off, Duke. He's mine, I saw him first," a third munchipod with a white ten gallon hat stepped from the crowd to Hick's right, his spurs jingling on the tattered hardwood floor.

"We'll see about that, Clint." Duke turned slightly to face his challenger.

"Uh, excuse me," Hick interrupted, "but I think it was him that saw me first." Hick pointed to a surly looking cowpoke, then another, adding, "of course it might have been him or him. I just can't be sure."

"I'll wager I saw him first," one cowpoke beamed.

"I'll take that bet, cause I saw him first," another argued.

Clint's hands hung tensely above his six guns. He squinted with his left eye while raising his right eyebrow, demanding, "Draw Duke."

Hick backed slowly from the line of fire in the direction of the bar. He kept an eye on the two duelers while remaining aware of erupting arguments among the crowd.

Duke's draw was like lightning. A single shot rang out and Clint's right arm, severed by the blast, flew back striking the wall before falling to the floor.

Seemingly unaffected by the loss of the arm, Clint began firing the gun in his left hand, missing each time.

Hick hurled himself over the bar and huddled close to the floor. A few paces away the bartender meticulously polished a beer mug with a dish towel. He was larger than an average munchipod, chubby, with a handlebar mustache twisted at the ends, and greased green hair parted down the middle. He wore a black apron over a puffy sleeved white shirt, with starched collar and cuffs.

Hick raised his head enough to see over the bar. The fight had spread. The gunfire sounded like a lit box of firecrackers. Chairs, bottles and severed arms and legs flew back and forth over the heads of the embattled mob.

A stray bullet shattered a bottle on the bar next to Hick. The contents ignited in a fireball singeing his cheek and sending him sprawling back to the floor. The flames set off two more bottles which flew like rockets across the room exploding against the walls. Suddenly the sound of a bugle blowing taps blasted above the clatter. The gunfire and noise ended, as the munchipods obeyed the bugle.

Once again Hick peered over the bar. The smoke began to clear, and the crowd parted for a middle aged green cowboy wearing a tin badge. He walked to the center of the room, with bugle in one hand, and six shooter in the other, as he surveyed the wreckage. "Quiet!" he demanded, tucking his bugle into his gun belt. He turned a piercing gaze on the crowd and waited for the noise to die. "Okay, who started it?"

The munchipods began to blame one another and chaos took root.

Drawing his gun the sheriff fired twice at the ceiling. "I said Quiet." Again the noise died.

"He started it." The bartender pointed an accusing finger at Hick, then resumed casually polishing his beer mug.

Hick straightened and gulped.

The sheriff turned his attention, and his six gun on Hick. "All   right,   come   along   peaceably."

Chapter Six

Hick peered through the cold steel bars separating the sheriff's office from the only cell block. The sheriff reclined in a wooden swivel chair with his feet crossed atop an oaken desk, his arms stretched leisurely behind his head, and his white hat lowered to cover his face. Behind him was a rifle rack with ten lever action rifles chained and locked. The walls were red brick with iron framed windows blackened by the evening darkness.

"So, what's the deal here?" Hick asked. "What are the charges, am I allowed a phone call?"

"Well," the sheriff drew a deep breath and let it out in a lazy fashion. "Soon as we find out who you belong to, you'll be turned over to them. If we can't determine whose slave you are, you'll most likely be assigned to the rock pile or sum'pin like that." He glanced at the keys hanging on the wall beyond Hick's reach, then back at Hick. "By the way, don't get any foolish ideas about escapin'. There is no way to escape from this here jail. Some fool alien escaped a while back by lifting the door off the hinges. We knew just how he did it – 'cause the dumb sucker left the door sittin' over there." The sheriff raised his hat and pointed to Hick's right. Lowering his hat he crossed his arms and reclined. "That dumb sucker ever come back here he'll hang." He yawned. "That's the penalty for escape; hangin'." His voice seemed to slow and soften, "We'll decide what to do with you tomorrow."

Hick watched the sheriff closely, as he began to nod off, fidgeting now and then and finally relaxing into an all-out snore. When Hick was certain the sheriff was asleep, he backed slowly across the cell to his cot below the barred window. Taking the communicator from his pocket, he whispered, "Hiroshi, come in, come in."

"Yeah, is that you Hick?" Hiroshi's voice lacked the muffled tin sound produced by the communicator.

Hick examined the communicator marveling at the advances in audio technology. Returning it to his lips, he whispered, "Where are you?"

"Dude, if I were a snake," Hiroshi replied.

Bewildered, Hick stared at the communicator and turned. He winced slightly, startled by Hiroshi's presence outside the barred window.

A smile crossed Hick's face as he leaned forward gripping the bars. "I take back almost every bad thing I ever thought about you." He started to clarify the *almost* but decided not to.

"Hey, you were bound to come around," Hiroshi whispered, "but lighten up on the mushy stuff, 'cause I'm not hero material, and you're not my favorite dude, okay? Now that we're straight on that, let's find a way to get you out of here. Quietly and carefully lift the door from its hinges."

"you can't do that anymore."

"Why not?"

Hick mimicked the sheriff, "'cause some dumb sucker did that once before and left the door sittin' over there."

Hiroshi struck his forehead with his palm and rolled his eyes upward. "Dude, did I forget to put the door back?" he smiled and shook his head regretfully. "If I'd put that back they'd think we could walk through walls, and they'd probably be worshiping us by now."

"What?" Hick squinted, "You lost me there."

"Uh, nothing. Forget the door, the question now is how to get you out of here?"

Once again Hick mimicked the sheriff, while pulling gently on the bars, "there is no way to escape from this here jail." Suddenly the barred window broke free from the brick frame, causing Hick to stumble backward still clutching the bars.

"Muffle the jokes, dude." Hiroshi smiled facetiously. "You're in big trouble now!"

Hick placed the bars on the cot. He turned and glanced at the sheriff snoring peacefully, and quickly climbed through the window into the alley.

From the alley the two men rushed to the dark city street staying in the shadows as much as possible until they reached the outskirts of town where they stopped to breathe.

"What are we going to do about fuel and repairs?" Hick asked.

"That's a tuff one," Hiroshi sighed, "We might make it into orbit on auxiliary, but we could run out of food and have to eat one of your animals. I'll radio back to Earth for repairs. Maybe I'll tell them we were struck by a meteor, that is, if you have no objections. One thing's for sure, we can't stay here. C'mon, find your inner gazelle."

"What?"

"Grow some wings, dude."

Their flight continued into the countryside, over the smooth rolling hills beneath the dim light of three fingernail moons. Once again they stopped to rest and get their bearings. In the distance the sound of a bugle split the silence.

"The posse!" Hiroshi's eyes widened and his tone took on a fearful quiver. "Come on, dude." He called out, leading Hick by several paces.

Looking over his shoulder, Hick saw flood lights scouring the countryside. The sound of the bugle grew louder with each passing second. Ahead lay the rocky crag where the ship was hidden.

"C'mon, faster!" Hiroshi shouted, looking back at Hick.

"I'm trying." Anger surged through Hick for his own inability to summon more response from his legs.

The thunder of steel hooves shook the ground as the posse gained on the two men, and the floodlights lit the landscape like a midday sun.

Hiroshi had multiplied his lead over Hick and offered no encouragement.

The ship was still a long way off and out of reach. Shots rang out and bullets whizzed past Hick's head. He spotted a tree and hurried to it for cover, while Hiroshi sprinted in a final effort to reach the ship.

The posse split into two groups. Half of them surrounded Hick at the tree while the other half captured Hiroshi before he could reach the ship.

Engulfed in a cloud of dust and light, Hick searched frantically for a way out but found none. A lariat flew over his head, encircling him, and tightening around his chest and arms. Another followed, tighter than the first.

"You little bastard dudes. I'll kill every last one of you," Hiroshi grunted, struggling against the rope, as a munchipod deputy dragged him behind a robotic horse towards the tree.

Another deputy draped two nooses over a high branch, under which they positioned the two men.

"All right boys," the sheriff beamed, "let's resolve this amicably. String 'em up!"

One of the deputies maneuvered his horse behind the men, fixing the nooses over their heads.

"Wait a minute!" Hick shouted, trying to sound authoritative amid doubts this could really be happening.

The sheriff reined his horse in close to the men and kicked Hick in the head. "Nobody told you to talk!" he growled.

"No one was ever hanged without last words," Hick blurted as though quoting scripture, "uh, it's the Code of the Old West!"

"That's no smack, dude" Hiroshi reaffirmed angrily, "you can't hang us without last words. It says so right in the code. Every cowdude knows that!"

Staggered by the statement, the sheriff and deputies looked at one another with uncertainty. The sheriff lifted his hat and scratched his head, "He's right. After all, what could it hurt." He turned to Hick. "All right, but make it quick!"

Chapter Seven

Stumbling for words, Hick began, "uh, real cowboys don't ride robotic horses!" He noticed anger and confusion building in the eyes of the posse, "Real cowboys ride bulls!" He forced a nervous nod, gaining momentum from the doubt his words had instilled. "You call yourselves cowboys, but I'll bet there ain't one of you that can ride a bull for eight seconds to save his life!"

The deputies looked at one another with astonishment. Slowly a fervor grew among them beginning with a mild grumble and growing to a mutual outrage.

"Silence," the sheriff called out, but the rabble grew louder. "Silence," he shouted again to no avail. Drawing his pistol, he fired two shots into the air and once again shouted, "silence!"

Only the echo of the gunshot and the sound of the bullet in its upward trajectory persisted.

Hick winced slightly, his ears ringing from the blast.

A confident expression formed on the sheriff's face, as he looked around at the astonished posse, appreciative of the reverence he'd gained.

Methodically he tilted the barrel of his pistol, blowing away the smoke before spinning it back into his holster. He leaned towards Hick resting his elbow on his saddle horn. "What the hell is a bull and where could we get one?"

The posse followed with a unanimous, "yeah!"

Hick released a tense sigh. He shot Hiroshi a look of satisfaction before turning his gaze back to the sheriff. "Let me clue you in on a little secret," he whispered loud enough for the posse to hear with all the charisma of a car dealer selling a lemon to a gangster, "I have a bull." He paused to allow the words to sink in. "Heck, I'll even be willing to provide my bull for the occasion if you'll agree to my wager."

"Wager?" the word echoed in unison from the eavesdropping posse, all of them leaning towards Hick, intent on gaining the smallest tidbit from the conversation.

Hick pretended to be surprised at their reaction. He glanced at Hiroshi, finding little tolerance in his expression, then back at the sheriff. "First of all, take these ropes off, and I'll tell you all about it."

"Boys, remove those ropes," the sheriff demanded with an optimistic but somewhat relenting tone.

Immediately the deputies whipped slack into the ropes and whirled them from the two men without dismounting.

Hick rubbed his arms where the ropes had restricted his circulation. "Well, here's the deal. I'll bet everything I got that there ain't a cowboy here who can ride my bull for eight seconds. If I win we get our freedom and you must help us repair our ship and provide us with fuel..."

"And if we win," the sheriff cut in, beaming with excitement, "we get to bring both of you out here and hang you amicably!"

The posse shouted joyously at the suggestion and fired pistols into the air.

Hiroshi gave Hick a look of disbelief and rolled his eyes in disgust. "Dude, we could make a break for it now," he whispered.

"You gotta' be kidding, they'd have us before we made it halfway to the ship. No! At least this way we have a chance. Just keep quiet and let me do the talking." Turning away from Hiroshi, Hick shouted, "wait a minute, I'm not finished yet." He waited for the noise to die before continuing. "If I win this wager, I want VIP treatment for the two of us."

"Sounds fair enough." The sheriff nodded. "Now where's that bull?"

Chapter Eight

The early morning air chilled Hick's face and arms. The sun seemed to promise warmth, and although it was slow to deliver, it offered a glimmer of hope in the wake of a hopeless situation. It gradually burned its way into the shadows and alleyways of the sleeping town.

The seemingly barren city sprang to life with the daylight as though some silent alarm had awakened the inhabitants. They came from nowhere yet everywhere to throng the board walkways and spill over into the streets. They watched with expressions of guarded amazement, Hick and Hiroshi leading the cattle, accompanied by the posse.

The two men forced themselves to wave and smile despite the cool reception. "We're the Grand Marshalls of this parade," Hick pointed out, "and our future depends on the impression we make with these," he hesitated, "well, whatever they are."

The deputies sat as tall as possible in their saddles looking hardened and distinguished. Each wore a bronze star on the chest and carried a lever action rifle. They all had gun belts with at least one pistol and holster. The twisted green handlebar mustache was popular with some, while the well shaven look suited others. Cowboy hats ranged in color and cleanliness. Some were flat brimmed, others, turned up in front in the old pony express style.

"Motley bunch of little bastard dudes, aren't they?" Hiroshi whispered through clenched teeth. He nodded towards the posse, while maintaining a solid smile, and continuing to wave to the onlookers. "I'd like to get my hands on that sheriff and strangle the green slime right out of him."

"You might get your chance." Hick rubbed a small painful bump on the side of his head where the sheriff had kicked him. He clenched his teeth momentarily. "I'd like some of that green slime myself, but let's establish some respect first." He pointed and waved to several children, all of whom immediately scampered and hid behind adults. "They say you can catch more flies with honey than with vinegar."

"Dude, recognize anybody you know? Hiroshi's sarcasm seemed to mount as he spoke. "That one over there reminds me of my aunt, Keiko, rotten witch." He forced a smile and waved. "They all have such sweet voices when they're young, but as they get older, they get coarse, smoker's voices."

"You lost me. You mean the munchipods?" Hick waved and smiled to the spellbound onlookers.

"No! Japanese women!" Hiroshi blurted.

"What?"

"Dude! Ya' had to be there!" Hiroshi shook his head and rolled his eyes.

Hick tried to focus on the Munchipods. *After all, Hiroshi was under a lot of stress.*

The crowd continued to grow, filling the street, parting to form a path as the procession approached. The news spread rapidly and one munchipod after another could be heard asking, "What are they?" followed by the elbow to the gut, and, "Ain't you never seen bulls before?"

With a raised hand and "Whoa," the sheriff brought the procession to a halt in front of the livery stable across the street from the city hall. "You two wait inside the stable until I return and call for you. Don't get any notions of trying to get away, cause my posse will be waiting outside."

"Wait," Hick called to the sheriff as the double wood doors were closing, "what happens next?"

"We have to wait for an emergency session of the Town Council," the sheriff replied, barring the doors from the outside.

After releasing the cattle to feed on a stack of hay, Hick and Hiroshi wondered about the stable. Sunlight filtered through cracks in the vertical wood walls providing enough illumination for the two men to see. Robotic horses, palomino, roan and appaloosa, stood like statues in stalls that lined one side of the structure. Harnesses and tack hung from nails on beams above the horse-gnawed boards.

"You know," Hiroshi's eyes lit up as he reached towards the appaloosa. "With a couple of these horses, you and I could…

"I wouldn't do that," Hick cautioned.

"Why?" Hiroshi cocked his head, a look of mockery in his eyes.

With the reflexes of a steel trap, the horse bit Hiroshi's hand, and then returned to its statue-like stance as quickly as it struck. Hiroshi drew back his hand growling in agony mixed with surprise.

"Ah, never mind," Hick said turning and lowering himself to the straw covered floor beside an empty stall.

A look of disgust filled Hiroshi's face. He sat down opposite Hick, painfully observing his reddened hand. The look slowly transformed to a sad smile laced with hopelessness and self pity. He forced a chuckle.

"What's so funny?"

"Dude, your face, it's covered with dirt."

"Yeah, well, so is yours." Hick felt his voice slip and waiver. He yawned and wiped moisture from his eyes with the backs of his hands.

Hiroshi shook his head. "Dude, I really screwed this one up." his words came slow, as though forced from his throat, "I know it's all me. My bad, my bad." Then he released it. At first it sounded like laughter. Hick too joined in a discharge of chortles which turned to piteous whines. Moments later the two were embraced at the neck crying like orphaned children.

"Dude, cut me some slack, here?" Hiroshi shouted, shoving Hick away.

"Me? What do you think you're doing?"

"I googled you, and a pic of you and that Charlene dude or dudess came up. I know what kind of guy you are." Hiroshi pointed an accusing finger at Hick.

Hick threw up his hands. "Don't worry about it, you're not my type."

"Likewise, dude." Hiroshi sat down opposite Hick.

"What if they can do it?"

"Do what?" Hick glanced up.

"What if they can ride your bull?" Hiroshi brushed hay from his pants.

"It's not as easy as you think." Hick tried to sound reassuring. "Bubba may look gentle enough, but once he's flanked he's a buckin' machine!"

"Flanked, what's flanked?" Hiroshi squinted, his anguish seemingly gone.

"We put a strap around his flank, makes bulls crazy. Might even put a spider under the rope."

"Spider? What do you mean, spider?"

"Just a little spur, it irritates them, makes 'em buck."

"Sounds cruel." Hiroshi's mouth dropped.

"Maybe so, but I want to get out of here alive, and if that's what it takes, I'm willing to do it."

"Count me in." Hiroshi nodded.

The double wooden doors opened and light streamed into the stable nearly blinding the two men. The sheriff shouted from the doorway, "get up, come with me and hurry up." His hands quivered in front of him with excitement. "The Mayor and town council will be here and I want to make a good impression, so you two be on your best behavior, ya hear? Don't go causing me any trouble now."

He led the two men across the street to a large white building with lap siding and a barn style roof. A white board sign hung by chains from the eves with *City Hall* in bold black letters.

The sheriff nodded for them to enter, then followed up the board steps into the building. The interior reminded Hick of an old time court room with rows of wood benches facing a varnished oak dais. Atop the dais were placards for the mayor and eight councilmen, with a gavel in the center beside the mayor's placard.

The sheriff guided the men to their seats on the left front side of the room and took a seat beside them. The remaining seats filled quickly with babbling green townspeople.

One by one the council members entered from a doorway behind the dais. They wore black pleated robes and looked very distinguished. Finally the mayor entered and stood behind his placard. He was balding and chubby, although it was hard to tell because of the way his robe covered him. His eyes scoured the room as he waited for silence to fall. When the noise persisted, he picked up the gavel and began to pound, demanding "silence!" The council members joined, reinforcing his demand, finally the room grew silent.

"This meeting is now in session!" the mayor announced. He turned to the council member to his right. "What is the first order of business?"

The councilman lowered his glasses. "The only order of business," he said, raising a piece of paper eye level, "is that the sheriff has asked for an emergency meeting of the council. He says it's of the utmost importance!"

The mayor's eyes fastened angrily on the sheriff. "You want to tell us, Sheriff, what the meaning of this is? Why have you called the council to an emergency session this time of the morning?"

The sheriff stood to his feet, removed his hat and held it against his chest. "Well Ralph…"

"That's Mr. Mayor to you, Sheriff!" The Mayor struck the dais with the gavel angrily. "Now what is the nature of this so called emergency?"

"I'm sorry, Mr. Mayor. The nature of this emergency is that an alien space ship landed, and…"

The crowd began to mutter, interrupting the sheriff.

"Shut up!" the mayor demanded, pounding the gavel. Once again the crowd fell silent. "Now, you were saying?"

"One of the aliens was taken into custody, but escaped."

"Escaped?" the mayor burst in, "I thought you remedied that problem!"

The exchange reminded Hick of a ping pong match.

The sheriff stretched his hands in front of him in a shielding gesture, "This was a very crafty alien, Mr. Mayor, but we recaptured them."

"Them?" The mayor nodded towards Hick and Hiroshi.

"Yes," the sheriff continued, "the second one broke the first one out. We were gonna' hang 'em, but..."

"But what?" The mayor's eyes enlarged. He leaned forward along with the council members, scrutinizing every word.

"But he pled the right to last words and offered a wager that none of us could ride his bull."

The crowd began to grumble. Again the mayor restored silence with his gavel, and leaning across the dais, squinted. "What the hell is a bull?"

The sheriff gulped. "Ahem, a bull is a big redish-brown and white animal with horns. It's got a big hump on its back and..." His eyes brightened. He tried to force a smile as he half turned with an air of excitement and pointed. "We got one right across the street!" Turning back, he motioned to Hick. "This alien says that real cowboys ride bulls instead of robotic horses in something called, 'a rodeo.' He says he's willing to bet everything that we can't ride his bull for eight seconds."

"You fool," the mayor shouted, "You could have had everything if you had hanged them!"

The sheriff dropped his head shamefully.

"Just a minute, Mr. Mayor," The council member to the mayor's right stood and leaned to whisper in the mayor's ear. The crowd grew quiet, as they listened for any tidbit they might salvage from the conversation.

Hick was able to pick out the phrases, "Tourist attraction, commerce, trade, political status and re-election gimmick." The Mayor's eyes fluttered at the councilman's every suggestion. With a slight jerk and a glow of optimism he turned his attention back to the sheriff. "What does this alien need in order to get started?"

The sheriff began to count on his fingers, "He wants something called a rodeo arena, he wants to be allowed to return to his ship nightly. He wants fuel and repairs. If we lose, he wants…"

The mayor struck the dais with his gavel and bellowed, "By all means, give him what he wants!"

Chapter Nine

"Where do you want this load of lumber, mister?" a buckboard driver called out.

Hick looked up from his blueprint table in the center of what was rapidly becoming the rodeo arena and gasped at the progress the munchipods had made since his last glance. "Put it over there." He pointed to his right.

The arena was one hundred yards long by fifty wide, with grandstands on both sides. An entry chute had been built for trapping the bull at the east end, with two exit gates, and a return chute at the west end.

In three days the munchipods had almost completed the arena, swarming over the grandstands and fences with hammers and handsaws like worker bees on a sugar high. Hick had scarcely drafted the plans before they became reality, and he knew that completion was not far off.

***

"Come one, come all," Hiroshi called out to the spellbound crowd, as he waved his cane high above his head. His black top-hat and long sleeved white shirt with arm garter added authenticity to his role as a carnival salesman, and for the first time since the ship landed he was enjoying himself. "See the one the only Bull." He turned and pointed the cane at the ten-foot placard behind him depicting Bubba with horns lowered, pawing the ground, fire flaring from his nostrils. "He moves--the earth shakes, he bellows, he breathes fire. One swat of his tail can wipe out an entire crowd of adult munchipods."

The crowd gasped and stepped back in unison.

"But not to worry dudes," Hiroshi continued, "'cause he's behind solid steel bars, and we all know how reliable they are." Hiroshi removed his hat and extended it upside down towards the crowd. "Just one ten dollar gold piece covers your admission. That's right, ladies and gentlemen, dudes and dudesses, up the steps and into the tent behind the sign." Hiroshi's hat filled quickly, as the crowd pressed forward. "Keep it moving now. Everyone wants to see the bull so don't be selfish. Take a quick look and move on."

***

The "Exhibit" was a success from the start and grew even more popular when Bubba ripped the arm from one of the munchipods and chewed it like cud with casual indifference, while the crowd watched with horror as the one armed munchipod screamed in agony.

An area three feet in front of Bubba's cage was roped off and signs were hung to prevent onlookers from getting too close, but this only presented more of a challenge.

Hick was both surprised and relieved to learn that the munchipod children had developed a taste for cattle droppings. The lack thereof had him worried the bull was constipated.

"Dude, we should bottle and sell the droppings." Hiroshi suggested, "after all these people are already full of..."

"No!" Hick eyes enlarged. "That just doesn't seem right, in fact it's downright indecent."

*

Word of the great beasts spread rapidly throughout the countryside, causing Munchville to grow and tourism to flourish. In three days the population had doubled. The City fathers were pleased and everyone looked forward to the rodeo. The mayor shared in the excitement and offered to give a speech at the opening ceremonies.

"I'd like to give you a hand too, mister, but I gotta wait till they grow back!"

Hick turned from his table and blueprints to the vaguely familiar voice. He recognized the armless munchipod beside him as one of the gunfighters from the saloon. "You're Clint, right?"

The munchipod nodded and smiled.

Hick couldn't help but notice the humility in the little gunfighter's face. A tinge of sadness and pity overwhelmed him.

Clint was a stark contrast to the overweening ego from the saloon several days prior. Hick hesitated, not wanting to call attention to Clint's handicap, but curiosity got the best of him, "'Grow back,' you say?"

Clint nodded and grunted a matter of fact, "uha."

"How long does that take?"

"About four weeks." Clint's lips quivered slightly and his tone saddened. "If there's any way at all I can be of service to you, just let me know."

Hick shook his head, a look of regret covered his face. "Well, I'm sorry, but I don't need anybody right now…

Just then a group of juvenile munchipods scurried in from the surrounding crowd. One of them jerked Clint's pants down, exposing his tiny green legs. The pranksters disappeared as quickly as they came, their high pitched giggles blending with the noise of the rabble .

Clint looked down at his thin green legs and began to sob. "Could you do a favor for me before I go?"

Hick nodded, trying to maintain a neutral expression despite his shock.

"Would you mind pulling my pants up?"

Hick helped him with his pants, for which Clint thanked him between sobs, before turning to leave.

"Uh…wait," Hick called out, "I could use a friend." He raised an index finger and shook it while searching for words, "and advisor. It pays, uh… one gold piece per day, and all you can eat."

Clint's mouth dropped and a glimmer of joy shown in his watery eyes, as he turned and leaned a stub of a shoulder towards Hick. A tiny hand protruded from the shoulder socket.

Hick hesitated not knowing how to shake the hand, concerned he might damage, or pull it off accidentally, but when the smile left Clint's face, Hick extended thumb and forefinger, and wiggled the minute appendage ever so gently.

"Agreed!" Clint blurted with a rapturous high-pitched chuckle.

"Hick nodded. "Your job will be to report to me everything you hear or see that might help me in any way. Be my eyes and ears. If you do well I'll give you a bonus. Oh, by the way, no drinking while you're in my employ."

"No drinking?" Clint grimaced. "Oh, all right!" An honest smile formed on his face. "Trust me, you won't regret it. I'll be the best employee you ever had."

Although Hick could see no value in hiring an armless employee, Clint was the first munchipod of whom Hick had taken a good impression. He wondered if Clint's attitude would change as his arms grew back, or if he would remain humble. Hick chuckled and shook his head.

The smile left his face as he noticed the sheriff approaching followed by a small crowd of dignitaries dressed in black tuxedos with top hats. He recognized them as the mayor and council members.

"His Honor, The Mayor would like a word with you, mister," the sheriff informed.

Hick sensed a meekness in his tone and a touch of respect that wasn't there when the little peace officer was about to hang him.

The sheriff gesticulated to the approaching mayor and council members, and then stepped to one side to make room for them.

"How do you do, Mr. Hick?" the mayor extended his hand.

Hick shook modestly, not wanting to seem obliging or opportunistic.

"I'm Mayor Ralph," he leaned forward, raised his free hand to the side of his mouth and whispered, "you can call me Ralph." Straightening, he motioned to the almost finished arena. "Are we ready for the opening ceremony yet?"

"We'll be ready as soon as the arena is finished!" Hick stated with all the assurance he could muster, wishing he could slow the progress.

"It appears the arena is complete!" the mayor returned matter-of-factly, raising and lowering his green eyebrows.

"How long will it take you to fill this place?" Hick motioned a challenging arm towards each of the grandstands, knowing it would take both time and advertising to bring in the crowd.

"Not long!" The mayor turned and nodded to the sheriff with a coy smirk.

The sheriff drew his bugle from his belt, raised it to his lips and blew reveille.

Streams of munchipods of all ages began to filter into the grandstands.

Mayor Ralph raised two fingers to his lips and blew a shrill whistle. "Boys, over here." he pointed to a newly built podium, complete with handrails, at one side of the arena. A group of munchipods gathered around it and carried it to the center. The mayor ascended the podium. One of the councilmen handed him a wireless mike. "Testing, one two three," he began. A shrill squawk sounded over speakers mounted high on posts above the arena then died out. "May I have your attention please," he continued, as the spectators filled the grandstands. "I am honored on this momentous occasion…"

Realizing the urgency of the situation, Hick hurried across the east end of the arena in the direction of the carnival exhibit. He exited through a chute which opened into a long corridor lined with sawdust and bordered on both sides by newly built corrals. He found Hiroshi absorbed with his new occupation, pointing his cane at familiar faces, further enticing the already anxious crowd.

"And you, little dude sir, you've seen the one, the only bull. Tell us what you thought of it."

The crowd became silent.

"It reminded me of Wild Bill's Galactic Dawg, only much bigger!" an excited munchipod spouted.

"There you have it dudes, a phenomenon greater than Wild Bill's Galactic Dawg! Whatever that may be," Hiroshi announced.

Hick stepped onto Hiroshi's podium and whispered, "we gotta get Bubba over to the arena, they're ready for us." Turning, he motioned to the crowd, "That's all for today, folks! But don't miss the rodeo."

The crowd began to grumble as they disbursed.

Turning back to Hiroshi, Hick smiled. "Well look at you, Slick. You got a regular three ringed circus going here, and you're the main act. Whoa, look at this chunk of change." He kicked a wooden box that was half full of gold coins at Hiroshi's feet. We'll just have to call you P. T. Barnum from here on out."

"Ya all come back now, ya hear," Hiroshi called to the exiting crowd, with his best pseudo-western drawl, which sounded odd mingled with a mild trace of his Japanese roots. "Yeah, Hick. That's me, dude, P-T. There is surely a sucker born every minute." Donning a serious expression, he added, "Ya know all that money won't do us much good if those little dudes can ride your bull."

"I picked up some added insurance at the general store today," Hick pulled a tube of axle grease from his pocket.

"Dude, that's cheating!!!"

"Not cheating at all. The only rules in this rodeo are that we make the rules, and the only requirement is that we win at any cost."

"Dude, you're making a better impression every minute. Help me get this box of gold into the cattle pen. We'll bury it in the straw and nobody will mess with it."

As the two men entered the tent they encountered a group of muddy-faced munchipod children extending long sticks between the bars of the cattle pen in order to retrieve manure. After running the children off, they buried the box of gold coin inside the pen. Hick gathered his lead rope and a hastily prepared flank strap. He snapped the lead rope to Bubba's nose ring and smeared the bull's back with axle grease while Hiroshi finished putting on clown makeup from something that resembled a small Halloween makeup kit.

"Dude, do rodeos really have clowns, or is this something you made up to make me feel stupid?" Hiroshi pulled his wide pink suspenders over his shoulders. His face was white and his nose bright red. His bright red lip line extended and curved upward several inches beyond his mouth giving him a false smile. Baggy, high water pants revealed his white poke-a-dot socks. His shirt was horizontally striped with purple and yellow. "Dude, how's my makeup, is my mascara too thick?" He chuckled.

"Nope. It's about right," Hick said, adding, "Don't forget your cane."

***

The mayor's voice seemed to grow louder as Hick led the bull down the long sawdust corridor towards the arena with Hiroshi close behind. The speech was followed by the blare of a brass and woodwind band playing a Souza march. The sound sent nervous chills up Hick's back. He turned and glanced at Hiroshi, who seemed equally nervous, fidgeting and tugging at the seat of his pants.

"It's not my bad," he growled, "These darn tight suspenders are causing these pants to creep up on me. I'm walking around with a perpetual wedgy."

When they reached the end of the corridor, Hick led Bubba into a narrow chute at the east end of the arena. He locked the bull in and rounded the chute. Climbing the fence from the outside, he tossed the flank rope over Bubba's back allowing the ends to fall just in front of the bull's back legs. He used Hiroshi's cane to reach under the bull and recover

.

the loose ends. After coupling the ends in a half hitch with a bow, he pulled it tight. Bubba began to step wildly, angered by the discomfort. Hick tugged the loose end. The cinch relaxed and Bubba began to calm just as Hick had hoped. "Perfect!" he nodded to Hiroshi seated atop the fence on the other side of the chute. "When I say *let her go*, pull that handle, and don't forget to pull this cinch release after the rider is thrown."

Hiroshi nodded back with an expression of uncertainty.

"Tell the mayor we're ready."

Hiroshi waved towards the arena and gave the thumbs up signal.

"It appears, ladies and gentlemen," the mayor announced from his podium, "that Mr. Hick and Mr. Hiroshi are ready for the first contestant."

A small green cowboy in chaps, and ten gallon white hat, jumped from the fence at the west end of the arena and sauntered proudly across the sawdust ground. As he neared, Hick recognized him as Duke, the gunslinger from the saloon brawl. Hick gently bit his lower lip. *For Duke he would give the cinch an extra tug.*

"This must be a tense moment for the two aliens," the mayor's voice shook with conviction over the loud speaker. His tone was somewhere between theatrics and old time southern preaching. He waved a solemn finger in the air and continued, "knowing that today they could lose everything, and that one solitary turn of fate will mean the difference between freedom and death at the end of a noose. Ahem…" He paused for a moment at a loss for words, then he pulled a folded paper from his vest pocket, opened it and began to read, "And if you forget all else, remember this, that as your mayor, I have done, and will continue to do all that is within my power to promote the commerce, trade, growth and happiness of this community. And I close with this thought: As you stand at the voting booth, remember the joy brought to you by this administration. Thank you ladies and gentlemen. And now without further adieu, I bring you Munchville's first RODEO!" He removed his hat and bowed.

The crowd went wild with enthusiasm.

The same group of munchipods that carried the mayor's podium to the center of the arena returned to hoist it high above their heads. They carried it out the main gate with the mayor clinging to a hand rail on top, waving his hat to the cheering crowd as he went.

Duke climbed the chute gate and peered over, "Are you ready for me yet?"

"Climb on!" Hick pointed at the bull's back.

"Looks like they're almost ready folks," an unfamiliar voice boomed over the loud speaker. Hick realized the microphone had been transferred to an announcer in the grandstands. He looked around but couldn't make out who or where the voice was coming from.

Duke climbed onto Bubba's back. The bull began to step about nervously.

Reaching between the boards, Hick pulled the cinch tight. Although restrained by the narrow chute, Bubba began to buck and snort.

Duke's eyes widened in fear, as he fumbled with his hands over Bubba's greasy hump, grabbing frantically for anything that might serve as a handle, but finding none.

Hiroshi flashed Hick a look of urgent humanitarian concern, "dude, aren't they supposed to have a rope, or reins, or something to hold onto?"

"Not in my rodeo!" Hick said with icy resolve, following with, "Let er go!"

Hiroshi tugged the handle, causing a weight to drop which in turn pulled the chute gate open. Bubba lunged into the arena bucking, kicking and snorting. Almost instantly Duke was thrown ten feet in the air and landed on his head. Bubba whirled and charged the little green cowboy, striking with his horns, thrusting this way and that.

Before Hick and Hiroshi could reach the bull, a tiny green arm flew one direction, and a leg the other. Hiroshi grabbed the quick release and the cinch fell from the bull's flank. Bubba's anger began to subside and after a few tense moments the two men were able to herd him into an exit coral and down a fenced corridor leading back to the chute.

Another cowboy was summoned. He took his place on Bubba's back dutifully with a look of frightened determination like a martyr to the guillotine. Hick recognized him as one of the posse members; the one that placed the noose over his head. He considered briefly how poetic justice comes about now and then.

Once again Hiroshi pulled the lever and the bull was released. The crowd went wild as Bubba spun and kicked creating a cloud of dust. The little rider fell to the ground head long. Hiroshi rushed in quickly to loosen the cinch, but Bubba swung and flailed wildly, narrowly missing Hiroshi's head with his right rear hoof. Hiroshi finally managed to release the cinch, but not before the rider was literally squashed and torn to bits. A stretcher crew gathered the scattered array of severed limbs tossing them onto the stretcher with the rest of the injured munchipod, while the two men herded Bubba from the arena and back to the chute.

"Whoa, dude, that was close," Hiroshi remarked between labored breaths, as he pulled himself back atop the chute fence. Once seated, he burst into uncontrollable laughter. "Did you-did you recognize that little dude?

That was one of those little deputies. It-it was just like whoosh and splat," Hiroshi threw his arms upward barely maintaining his balance before bursting once again with laughter, "and it ended just like that! Dude, they're still picking up the pieces!"

Hick noticed the sweat draining from Hiroshi's reddened brow, and he knew this was a mental release as well as the end of a physically exhausting ordeal. He too felt a great release of pressure along with comfort in watching the carnage, although he kept it to himself.

The announcer called for a third rider, but the would-be contestants, most of them posse members, sat atop the far fence shaking their heads in refusal.

Hick slid from the fence to the ground, he knew it was over, and he and Hiroshi had won.

Hiroshi jumped from the fence and patted Hick's back, a look of relief on his soiled clown face. "Dude, I was hoping the sheriff would ride." He chuckled adding, "Next time, dude, you get to be the clown, 'cause I'm sellin' popcorn in the grandstands!"

***

Charlotte McHenries leaned her hulking frame against the hatchway and peered angrily at the pilot and co-pilot. "You mean to tell me that after months in space we're nowhere near our destination? You're supposed to be the fastest, most efficient carrier, and now you need to make an intermediate stop on some planet for oxygen?"

"Yes Ma'am," replied one of the pilots, "We've exhausted most of our onboard oxygen supply running at warp speed, and we'll have to make a pit stop on a nearby planet to replenish.

"You men are all alike, you make promises that you never intend to keep," Charlotte ranted.

"Ma'am, we've been over this repeatedly since we left Earth. You were promised that you would reach your destination in a timely fashion, and believe me Ma'am, if we could get you there any sooner, we would."

The hatch door slammed and the two pilots looked at one another with relief. Neither dared to speak until the vibration of Charlotte's footsteps, down the titanium passageway, diminished to a mild patter. "That woman gives new meaning to the word "weird," said the pilot.

"I'm not convinced she's really a woman! Never saw one that massive. She could play professional football." said the co-pilot.

The pilot grimaced and shook his head. "I don't even want to go there."

"So she's chasing a lover across space with a cargo of ten thousand virtual goggles?" The copilot rubbed his chin, a baffled expression on his face.

"Yeah, the goggles are supposed to help her image."

"How is that possible?"

"Don't ask me." The pilot shrugged. "I just drive spaceships."

Chapter Ten

"Delayed?" Hick shouted, leaning across the sheriff's desk. "What do you mean delayed?" Hick could see the fear in the sheriff's small green eyes as he sprang to his feet and backed away from the desk, sliding his chair behind him.

"There's no reason to get upset." The sheriff made a calming motion with his hands. "I'm sure we can work this out to everyone's satisfaction."

Hiroshi's black shirt, hat, and boots, combined with the mounting contempt in his eyes to give him the look of an outlaw. He pushed Hick aside and hammered the desk with his fist. "Dude, we had a deal! A bet! You lost, we won! It's time for you to pay, and I mean now!"

"J-just look on the bright side, boys." the sheriff swallowed with difficulty and continued, "a-at least you're not swingin' from that tree, and in another month you'll have your rocket fuel and be on your merry way."

Hick knew it wasn't the sheriff's fault. He was simply the middle man doing what he was told. Reluctantly he nodded. "You got a point there."

Hiroshi turned to Hick. "Point? Dude!"

Hick wiped spattered saliva particles from his face.

"There's no point here!" Hiroshi leaned forward again hammering the sheriff's desk. "Dude, I want rocket fuel or I want green blood."

Hick placed his arm in front of Hiroshi's chest and tried to hold him back, "Let's talk for a minute."

Labored breaths passed between Hiroshi's teeth. The veins in his neck pulsed to an enraged rhythm.

"Calm down. Let's talk about this." Hick waited a moment for Hiroshi's anger to subside. Placing a hand on Hiroshi's shoulder, he guided him from the sheriff's office onto the board walkway. "What's got into you, anyway? I hardly know what to expect from you anymore. Get a-hold of yourself."

"Dude, I'm a-hold of myself," Hiroshi answered sarcastically, as he jerked his arm away. "I'm playing good alien, bad alien."

Hick shook his head in disgust and raised a threatening right forefinger. "I'm getting sick of your attitude, and I have half a notion to change it for you."

"Alright mister tough dude." Hiroshi tossed his cowboy hat to one side and backed into a karate stance. "I'm not the only one who needs an attitude adjustment, and I'm the dude who can adjust yours for you."

"This is ridiculous." Hick threw his hands up. "I don't want to hurt you, and I don't have anything to prove."

"Dude, you think you could hurt me? Give it your best shot!"

Hiroshi's foot seemed to come from nowhere, striking Hick in the gut, then on the cheek, causing him to stagger backwards. "Alright Hero." Hick felt rage building behind his eyes. He stepped from the walkway onto the street, checking his cheek for blood. "Let's see if you can run with the big dogs."

Hiroshi marched to the street opposite Hick, stretching his arms confidently as he moved within striking distance. His pose seemed relaxed and natural with a minor springing movement. "Dude, the name's Hiroshi! Only friends call me Hero."

A crowd of munchipods had already gathered to watch the fight. "My money's on Mr. Hick!" one said.

"I'll go two to one on Mr. Hiroshi," another challenged.

"You're on!" the first munchipod drew his wallet.

"I can't tell them apart," a third complained. "They look alike to me!"

"Hick is the one with the white shoelaces."

"Okay, I'll bet on him."

Hick lifted his hands chest level, leading with his left. He stood with his left foot forward, heels raised, teeth clenched, every unnecessary muscle relaxed. He could duck, lunge, punch or kick from his well balanced position, and he knew that habit born of practice and instinct would serve him well.

His next move depended on Hiroshi. He felt the joy he had known in the ring. He could hear a bygone crowd chanting his name, calling for blood. He shook his head vigorously, commanding his focus on the present. He didn't want to hurt Hiroshi. He would not allow his instincts to dominate his senses, but he would not lose. Hick locked into Hiroshi's gaze. He saw misguided confidence. He moved within range of Hiroshi's feet, provoking action.

Hiroshi sprang with a shout, turning horizontally, kicking with his right foot.

Hick moved his head just out of reach and watched the foot pass. Hiroshi regained balance on his right foot and followed with a left roundhouse. Hick dropped to a one-legged squat. Swinging his left leg, he swept Hiroshi's right ankle and toppled him backwards. Hiroshi threw his legs upward. His body followed, bringing him to his feet, but Hick met him with a solid right elbow, knocking him back to the ground.

"You had enough Hero, or you want more?"

Hiroshi held his nose and gazed angrily up at Hick.

"You got your licks in," Hick turned his reddened swollen cheek so Hiroshi could see. "Just remember two things; if you decide to continue. This is my game, and I won't be responsible for what happens to you."

Hick turned to the crowd of munchipods who had gathered to gamble. "Give that money back now." He shook an angry hand at them. "And don't you ever bet on Hiroshi and me again."

A hush fell over the startled gamblers. They obeyed and disbursed quickly.

***

That night the reflection of flames danced on the spaceship's shiny outer hull and shadows flickered on the surrounding rocks. Sparks from the campfire rose towards a dark green star-filled sky and three full moons.

The pain of being stranded on a hostile planet had eased, and the two men celebrated with marshmallows roasted on sticks and beer which Hiroshi had saved for a special occasion.

"I can't get over the look on that little dude's face when I cut the bull lose." Hiroshi's marshmallow caught fire. He pulled it from the flames, turning the stick to burn it evenly on all sides before blowing it out. "I like 'em like that." He said as he blew gently to cool it. "His expression is permanently filed in my mental photo album on my most hilarious pics page." Placing his lips around the marshmallow, Hiroshi pulled it from the stick. His eyes enlarged with pain, and he scrambled for the open bottle of beer in the green sand beside him, spilling it twice before dowsing his burning mouth.

"Yup," Hick chuckled, feeling a mild buzz from the beer. "I'm not sure which one you mean, but they both had priceless expressions." He took a bite from a lightly browned marshmallow on a stick and followed it with beer. "After I was sure they couldn't ride Bubba, I was hoping more of them would give it a try."

"Dude, I was thinking the same thing, but I wasn't enthused about being the clown or pulling off the cinch." Hiroshi leaned back on his elbows in the sand and glared at the sky. "Dude, what comes to mind when you think of Earth?"

A faraway glimmer flickered in Hick's eye, followed by a painful squint. He shook his head vigorously. "Ah, I don't even want to go there."

Hiroshi chuckled. "Dude, if that Charlene was stuck in my hard drive, I wouldn't click on it either." He raised a clenched fist, squinted and growled in a nasal monotone, "Dude, fight the urge!"

"Charlotte's not the face I see when I think of Earth. Charlotte was a brief encounter, a mistake caused by this." Hick held up the bottle.

"What happened?"

Hick felt a deep sadness welling within, "The girl I loved left me for another guy."

Hiroshi rubbed his nose and smirked. "Dude, don't tell me you beat her up!"

"No, I'm a pacifist by nature." Hick smiled.

"How 'bout the guy?"

"He cold cocked me with a pistol before I had the chance to do anything."

"Sounds like he knew more about you than you did about him." Hiroshi tipped his beer, holding a mouthful while he chuckled.

"You could be right." Hick placed another marshmallow on his stick and held it over the fire. "The thing that bothers me most is they took my dog with them when they left."

"Any idea where they are now?"

"I wonder all the time where she is and what she's doing?"

Hiroshi's face went blank. "Dude, are you referring to the dog or the girl?"

"Both."

***

A whip cracked on the stage near the toe of Roni's high-heel shoe. She winced and crossed shivering arms over a red low-cut silk dress and sobbed. "I don't understand what you want from me. Why are you doing this to me?"

"I told you I wanted a song." A stocky munchipod, stood at the edge of the stage in buckskin clothes and hat, growling as he twisted one end of his handlebar mustache. "What kind of song has words like, *I want to feel the beat of your body close to mine?"* He mimicked with a falsetto. Don't you know, *Get along little Cindy?* or *Swannee River?* Now if you can't sing I'll have Weasel whip you again or I might just end up using you for target practice." He turned to the burly man seated at the bar room table to his right. "I thought you said she could sing, Boo."

"It's Bo if you please, Mister Wild Bill," the burly human raised cuffed hands in an explaining gesture.

"I'll call you whatever I dern well please, 'cause you're my slave." Wild Bill fingered a Sharps-style rifle leaning against the stage beside him. "I captured you fair and square when your spaceship crash-landed. Now I dern well prefer Boo to Bo, and don't you ever sass me again."

"Yes Mr. Wild Bill."

A wiry munchipod, dressed in black leather, holding a coiled whip released a loud, high pitched laugh. He was joined by chortles and giggles from five of Wild Bill's munchipod mountain-men scattered throughout the bar.

Wild Bill turned back to Roni. "We haven't got all day. Now sing."

In a shaky voice she began, "what's your problem, cowboy..."

Wild Bill listened to the first verse before interrupting, "That's enough." He turned to his men. "It still ain't singing, but it's an improvement, so drink up boys 'cause we're headin' for Munchville." He took a mug of beer from the table in his right hand, while lifting the rifle with his left, and fired a shot through the ceiling. Smoke from the blast filled the room and the sound vibrated the walls.

Weasel led the men in a round of ridiculing laughter and yeehaws while particles of wood and dust fell from overhead.

Chapter Eleven

From behind a counter in the waiting room, a tiny green secretary informed the two men, "The mayor will see you now." She removed her head phones and rounded the counter to show Hick and Hiroshi into the mayor's office.

"Come in boys," Mayor Ralph summoned from behind a large wooden desk. The office was three floors up with wood paneled walls and a large window overlooking Munchville's streets and saloon. "Pull up a chair and sit down boys."

Hick sat in one of the hard wood chairs facing the mayor while Hiroshi spun his chair and straddled it. He crossed his arms on the back of the chair, tipped his hat and allowed his boots to settle with a slight knock on the hardwood floor.

"You boys like a cigar?" The mayor raised the lid on a box of fine cigars and slid them across his desk.

"No thanks," Hick said, anxious to get down to business.

"Naa, dude, got chew." Hiroshi opened his lower lip to reveal an ugly wad of chewing tobacco.

Mayor Ralph blinked several times and fastened his eyes on his desktop. "So, what brings you boys here today?"

"Dude, we want repairs and rocket fuel!" Hiroshi stood and shook his fist.

"Just a minute, Hiroshi," Hick cautioned, placing his hand on Hiroshi's shoulder and seeing him to his seat. "Mr. Mayor, as noted at your council meeting, we agreed to perform the rodeo in exchange for fuel and repairs if we won. Well sir, we won, and so far you haven't lived up to your part of the bargain."

"I can understand your feelings boys, and I intend to make it up to you in every way." His voice was soft yet firm. He raised his right index finger. "But as you know the people here don't take kindly to aliens. There is still a large faction that would like to see you hang or worse." He paused to light a cigar. "I am the only thing standing between you and the noose. Cross me, and I step out of the way. Do you catch my drift?"

Hick glanced at Hiroshi then back at the mayor. "Yes."

"First," the mayor continued, shaking the cigar at the two men, "we want a real rodeo. Not a sham of a rodeo like the one you arranged. It would seem you've taken us for fools. A couple of cowboys riding a solitary bull is not a rodeo. We want a rodeo with all the trimmings!"

"All the trimmings?" Hick scratched his head and leaned forward wondering what insight the mayor might have and where he'd gained such knowledge.

"Yeah, you know, calf roping, bulldogging, a wild west show." He raised an eyebrow and reasserted, "All the trimmings!"

"Dude, that's hilarious," Hiroshi volunteered with a smile to match a fake southern drawl. "Hick and I were just discussing that very thing. Weren't we, Hick?"

"As a matter of fact!" Hick nodded.

"Well, here's what we got, boys." The mayor took a hand full of papers from a desk drawer and held them up one by one, displaying schematic drawings. "We're presently building robotic calves and steers in several designs and prototypes, along with a new breed of robotic horse. We've got horses for bucking, horses for cutting. You name it we've got it. Wild Bill will be here with his Wild West Show. And you, of course will offer bull riding." He glanced back and forth between Hick and Hiroshi as he spoke. "After the rodeo, you're free to go, and I will provide fuel and repairs to your ship. Are we clear on this matter?"

Hick looked at Hiroshi, then back at the mayor and nodded. "Yes, we're clear."

"Oh, and one more thing." The mayor raised a finger, bringing Hick and Hiroshi to a halt somewhere between a sitting position and a stance. "We want to know how real cowboys dance."

"Dance?" Hick queried, still pondering the upcoming rodeo.

"Dance!" The mayor reasserted with raised eyebrows and wrinkled forehead.

"No problemo, dude," Hiroshi straightened, "Hick here, is a professional when it comes to cowboy dancing, or *Western Dance* as it's called." Hiroshi leaned towards Hick, patting his back and smiling, while allowing a drop of chew to dribble down his own chin.

Hick shook his head frantically. "I don't dance, I'm...."

"Dude, he's modest," Hiroshi cut in, "Hick is actually one of the universe's foremost authorities on Western Dance, aren't you Hick?" He slapped Hick's back.

"Wonderful! Wonderful!" The mayor applauded, "We'll look forward to you teaching us how real cowboys dance. The dance will be in the town square on the first night of the rodeo. Just tell us what you need and we'll get it for you."

***

The Munchville saloon was quiet and poorly lighted, offering a good refuge from the warm afternoon sun. The large room was almost empty with the exception of Hick, Hiroshi and Clint seated at a table, and the bartender who stood behind the bar polishing mugs.

Clint's limbs had grown considerably since the Rodeo. Little arms and elbows protruded from his shoulder sockets. His hands wiggled from time to time, inciting silent laughter from Hiroshi which he hid by feigning a yawn or rubbing his nose.

"So these delays are fabricated?" Hick paraphrased Clint's words as he took an apple-like fruit from a bowl on the table and polished it on the front of his blue tee shirt. He didn't want to put words in Clint's mouth, but he and Hiroshi had met with Clint for one purpose; to gather information.

"I don't know what fabricainted means." Clint said with a look that fell somewhere between a squint and a grimace.

"He means they just made it up so they could keep us here, little dude." Hiroshi reached to his right and patted Clint's back.

Clint forced a burp and a smile. "Yeah, word is that you're good business and the Mayor and city counsel plan to keep you here as long as they can."

"Good work, Clint." Hick smiled through his disappointment, to let Clint know he had done well despite the nature of the tidings. Reaching into his pant pocket Hick drew out ten gold pieces. "Here's a bonus." He slid them across the table to Clint.

"Here, little dude." Hiroshi said, sliding him ten more.

"By the way." Clint shot Hick a look of innocence. "I haven't had a drink in weeks. For a beer-just one beer, I'll tell you more." He tried unsuccessfully to gather the scattered coins with his tiny hands and arms.

"Sure." Hiroshi nodded, turning towards the bar. "Bartender, one beer."

"Just a minute here." Hick's gaze was piercing. "Have you been holding out on us? You agreed to tell us everything for a fee. Now that you've received that and more, you're asking for another bonus to tell us what you should have told us to start with."

"Oh no." Clint shook his head meekly. "This has nothing to do with you or your situation. It's…"

"Dude, it's just interesting information, that we should know." Hiroshi offered a matter-of-fact nod in Clint's defense. Turning back to the bar he called out, "Hey bartender dude, make that two beers." Hiroshi helped Clint gather the coins into a money pouch which he placed in the chest pocket of Clint's vest.

"Two beers!" the bartender announced, standing at Hiroshi's left with two icy mugs.

"Muchos graciendos, dude." Hiroshi slid one mug to Clint, taking a whiff of the other, he wrinkled his nose and pushed it aside. "Smells like paint thinner."

Clint leaned forward, trying to grab the beer, but his arms proved too short. Giving up, he lowered his lips to the foam and steadied the mug with his little hands, slurping and swallowing. "Oh that's good," he said with a burp and a gasp, his mouth covered with a frothy mustache. "There's a rumor, Wild Bill's comin' to town. Word is he's upset cause you've been takin' all his business. Say's if he can't deal with ya', he'll feed ya' to his Galactic Dawg."

"W-what's this?" Hick straightened. "That hardly sounds legal. How could anyone get away with such a thing?"

"Wild Bill pretty much does whatever he wants. He's known for bein' above the law. He has some alien slaves, they're the same variety as you. He treats 'em pretty bad too." Clint leaned forward for another sip of beer.

"Dude, let me help you," Hiroshi offered, lifting the mug and tilting it against Clint's' lips. He lowered the mug when clint's eyes enlarged.

With a gulp and a burp Clint continued, "I'm not sure how he gets away with it. He either destroys the evidence or buys out the law. Crowds pay a bundle just to see some of the illegal exhibitions he puts on, and that Galactic Dawg of his is a big attraction."

"What about these alien slaves he has? Just how did he get them?" Hick cocked his head slightly in order to hear better.

"Word is their spaceship crash landed. That's how he got them and the Galactic Dawg. He keeps them caged up and uses them for wild west shows and carnival tricks, him and his henchman, Weasel." Clint's eyes returned fondly to the beer.

"Weasel?" Hiroshi helped Clint to another drink.

Clint swallowed. "Yeah, Weasel is Wild Bill's right hand man. He's deadly with a whip. They say he can whip a gnat off a chigger's butt at five yards!" Clint glanced towards the swinging doors. "Well, speak of the devil, there he is now! That's Weasel."

Hick and Hiroshi followed with their eyes as a wicked looking munchipod strode through the swinging doors into the saloon. He was dressed in black, from his hat and vest to his cowboy boots. He was a head taller than the average, slim and wiry. His green face was scarred and tough looking. Under his arm he carried a coiled bull whip. As he stepped up to the bar, he glared at the bartender and demanded, "Where would I find an alien by the name of Hick?"

The bartender pointed and casually resumed polishing a glass.

Weasel strode to within seven feet of the table and stopped. Placing his right hand on the whip handle, he fastened his eyes on Hick and said in a menacing voice, "hear you've done well for yourself, Alien!"

Hick offered no reply, but took another bite of the fruit.

"Wild Bill is awaitin' outside for ya'. He has an offer to make ya'."

"Dude, drink your beer, this'll grow your arms out." Hiroshi raised the almost empty mug of beer to Clint's lips and tilted it for him. Clint began to drink.

"I'm talking here!" Weasel demanded, uncoiling the whip.

A crack rang out and the mug flew from Hiroshi's left hand, spilling beer on his new western outfit.

"Dude! You hit me, you little cur!" Hiroshi picked up the empty mug with his right hand and hurled it at Weasel. The mug struck Weasel in the forehead, toppling him backward to the floor where he landed with a solid thump and laid motionless.

"Dude," Hiroshi moaned painfully, shaking and blowing his fingers.

"Nice shot," Hick offered, knowing the compliment would bring little relief. He rose to his feet and started towards the swinging doors.

Hiroshi followed but paused over Weasel's unconscious form. "Souvenir, dude," he growled jerking the whip from Weasel's hand.

The bright sunlight nearly blinded Hick as he stepped through the swinging doors onto the board walkway. Parked in the street was a buckboard wagon drawn by a team of robotic mules. A stocky munchipod, clad in buckskin sat on the seat holding a buffalo rifle with barrel pointed upward. He was weathered and tough looking with a long green handlebar mustache. In a barred cage in the back of the wagon was a big black and tan dog. Her large broad head and heavy muscular build gave her a formidable appearance. She snarled and growled at the crowd of curious onlookers gathered along the sidewalks.

Hick noticed the crowd watching his every move in silent anticipation. He sensed a showdown was in the air. He heard the squeak of the swinging doors behind him, as he stepped from the walkway to the street, and he knew Hiroshi and Clint were close at hand.

A gunshot rang out and faded, giving way to the sizzle of a lead slug in it's upward trajectory.

"That's far enough, alien!" With one hand the munchipod on the seat of the wagon lowered the smoking barrel of his rifle until it pointed directly at Hick. "The way I see it you have a choice to make, Alien. Give me your bull and cows, and I'll fix your spaceship so's you can get outta' town, or I'll feed you to my Galactic Dawg! Now which will it be?"

"Sounds like a fair offer. Take the repairs, give him the cattle." Hiroshi whispered.

"Not so fast." Hick motioned with his hand. "I may know something he doesn't know."

A single bark from the Rottweiler followed by the wag of a stubbed tail sent Hick's mind reeling. He stood for a moment shaking his head. "How could this be?" A second bark reminded him he needed to act. He pointed a finger back at Wild Bill and shouted, "You turn that dog loose, and she'll sit on my lap!"

"Mister, you don't know what you're askin' for. I watched this dawg maul an alien like you."

"I'll bet my bull and cows against your dog that what I say is true. She'll sit on my lap and lick my face!"

"Are you sure about this, dude? Hiroshi's words carried a tone of desperation.

"No," Hick leaned back and whispered, "but I think I know the difference between a wagging tail and a threatening growl when I see one, and he doesn't,"

"You're on." Wild Bill climbed to the back of the buckboard and onto the cage. "Everybody back except for you, alien," he demanded, pointing a confident finger and grinning sadistically.

The crowd rushed to safety, huddling together behind the hitching posts on both sides of the street.

Hick positioned himself a few yards behind the buckboard and sat down in the street facing the cage.

"This will be the easiest bet I ever won." Wild Bill unlocked the cage. "Are you ready?"

Hick nodded.

Wild Bill lifted the latch and pulled the door open. The crowd gasped as the large Rottweiler lunged from the cage onto the street. Their fear turned to surprise when the dog jumped joyfully onto Hick's lap and began licking his face.

"Sit," he instructed, running his hands over her face and neck, examining her markings. "Good girl. You're just like my Uggy Dog. In fact--that will be your name from now on."

The munchipods marveled at the way Uggy Dog obeyed Hick. Hick rewarded her with a hug, of which she took advantage, smothering him with slobbery kisses, and forcing him onto his back. He pushed her to one side and rose to his feet, proudly wiping dog slobber from his face with his sleeve. He tried to shout, "C'mon Uggy Dog," but the words, hindered by a lump in his throat sounded more like a squeal. Uggy Dog understood and followed, jumping against his leg with puppy-like exuberance.

Wild Bill slammed the cage door, cursing and shouting, "Nobody makes a fool of Wild Bill and gets away with it. You'll   pay,   you'll   pay!"

Chapter Twelve

Although overjoyed at winning the dog, Hick remained troubled at the idea of cowering to the mayor's demands.

He reminded himself that in order to survive on Planet M, one must accept life as though it were a game; a game that had to be played by a new set of rules; rules by which one offered no quarter and spared no expense to win.

The next move in the game was to learn to dance. He began by scouring computer files and video disks, in the ship's lounge, for anything that might contain information on western dance. He settled on some old videos from the country western era, around the year 2000. The disks had been kept more for historical significance than entertainment. They contained footage of groups of people stepping, swaying and clapping. The steps were easy to learn and therefore perfect for the occasion.

Hick hoped Mayor Ralph would not discover the music was out of style. *After all, just because it was out dated by earthly standards didn't mean it had to be out of style in Munchville. Besides, the munchipods would never know the difference.*

He wondered how the mayor knew about calf roping and bull dogging. *He must have an outside source. Would the same source tell him the music and dance was old and antiquated?* Hick quickly dismissed the thought; he would cross that bridge if and when he had to.

He began to practice the steps alone in front of the video screen to a song called *Achy Breaky Heart*, while Uggy Dog watched with curiosity from across the lounge. Hick repeated each movement aloud in order to memorize the sequence; "back right-left, right and stomp, hip rocks and hold, quarter turn-stomp and half turn." He felt a little silly at first, never having danced, but after a couple of hours he settled into the movements. He even added his own graceful swing and sway to make it look professional. "Right vine and stomp-clap." He'd always hated dancing. It seemed silly getting out on a crowded floor and wiggling around with a group of people. Perhaps if he'd learned to dance back on earth Roni would not have left.

"Dude, I can't tell what it is, but it looks like you're gettin' the hang of it." Hiroshi stood in the hatchway with a twenty dollar smirk on his face. "Or should I say, you're gettin' the swing of it? Yeehaw!"

Hick tensed, missing a beat or two. He forced himself to continue, his movements less fluid, more sudden. "This here is country western dance," he said, trying to sound southern, an air of resentment mingled with embarrassment in his voice. "It's closely related to that old rock an' roll, or whatever you call it. You'd better learn this too if you don't want us to look like a couple of greenhorns who don't know what they're doin'."

Hiroshi nodded and fell in beside Hick, trying to imitate his every movement right down to the un-relaxed butt swinging and hip swaying.

"My mother forced me to take hipno-dance lessons as a kid."

"Hipno-dance?" Hick almost lost his step.

"Yeah, dude. It was a teaching technique which used hypnosis to teach kids who refused to dance. I don't remember it, but I'm told I passed. I've even been told that I get up and dance every time I hear a rock beat, but that's a pack of lies. Of course if it did work, we could learn this without even trying. Then we could open a dance studio? Maybe find ourselves a couple of little green babes and settle down?" Hiroshi chuckled while following a split second late on each movement."

"I'm seriously trying to concentrate here and you're not helping. Hipno-dance!" Hick scoffed under his breath.

Hiroshi began adding a kick here, a sway there, and a wiggle at the end of each step.

Hick stopped abruptly, his eyes enlarged. "I can't do this if you're going to do that."

"Do what, dude?"

"That kick. That-that little wiggle." Hick rolled his eyes. "It's bad enough you got me into this, with, 'Hick is a foremost dance authority,' but now you come in here and ruin my practice."

"Let it out, dude, release your suppressed emotions. They say it's good for the inner dude."

"Aaaaah." Hick growled.

"Good, good dude. Hold that thought. Don't mind me. I'll just watch. Pretend I'm not here, and remember, breathe deeply." Hiroshi sat down in the recliner and began to pet Uggy Dog.

"Would you shut up!" Hick paused, enunciating each syllable.

Hiroshi offered a thumbs-up, smiled and nodded.

Hick resumed dancing, completing one additional song, a Brooks and Dunn number, in order to keep Hiroshi from thinking he had influenced his decision to quit.

Ejecting the disk, Hick carried it with the others to a cabinet along the bulkhead for safe keeping. He tucked the disks neatly onto an eye-level shelf beside a metal box labeled, *Hull Repair Kit,* and closed the door. Half-turning, he intended to say something to Uggy Dog when the words exploded in his mind.

"Dude, what's wrong?" Hiroshi squinted and shook his head.

"Hull Repair Kit," Hick said, too stunned to move.

"Dude, you sound like the tin man askin' for an oil can!" Hiroshi shook his head. "Let me see!" He forced his way past Hick and opened the cabinet, "Hull repair kit." His expression lacked emotion. He closed the cabinet and repeated, "hull repair kit."

Hick turned and reached for the cabinet door, but Hiroshi pushed his hand aside.

"I saw it first!" Hick pushed him back and took the box from the shelf. Setting it on the countertop, he flipped the latches and lifted the lid. Inside he found several sheets of sand paper, a tough foil made of titanium alloy, a bottle marked "solvent," along with two tubes of epoxy, and a page of instructions. "This is a hull repair kit?" Hick was ready to close the box when Hiroshi stepped in.

"Dude, it's worth a try!"

"You're right. After all we don't have much to lose and everything to gain." Hick nodded.

"Here, you take the box and get the stepladder. I'll open the waste door." Hiroshi's eyes were filled with mindless hope as he handed Hick the repair kit.

Hiroshi opened the waste door from the cockpit controls, while Hick took a step ladder from a utility closet. They met outside the ship where Hiroshi positioned the ladder under the waste door and climbed within easy reach of the hole in the fuel tank. Hick handed him a sheet of sand paper from the box and glanced over the instructions.

"It says here, 'The surface must be sanded and wiped free with solvent of all paint, dirt and oil. After the surface is prepared, mix equal amounts epoxy resin and hardener and apply to the titanium foil patch. Press the patch over the punctured surface. When the patch is dry it will withstand pressures of one hundred thousand pounds and heat in excess of two thousand degrees Fahrenheit." Hick squeezed equal parts of the resin and hardener onto the titanium patch, and began to mix with an applicator from the repair kit.

"Dude, that dog has taken to you quickly." Hiroshi paused from sanding, and pointed at Uggy Dog, leaning on Hick's leg.

"She's the spitting image of the dog I had back home. She used to ride on my tractor with me. They could almost be twins. In fact if I didn't know better, I'd say this is the same dog."

"Dude, I hate to disillusion you, but she can't be the same dog." Hiroshi stared at the dog. "Consider all the planets in space. It's impossible that your lost dog would turn up here. Chances are she's a survivor from a wrecked earth ship. It's totally psychological; she's lost her human master, who probably looks like you, at least in contrast to these little green people. You, like the dog, are marooned on a planet, heart sick, destitute, in need of companionship. To you, she's your beloved Uggy Dog." Hiroshi resumed sanding. "To her, you're her master. Dude, it's a psychological substitution, simple as that. Dude, you took a chance calling Wild Bill's bluff. In fact, I hardly think it was a bluff."

Hick allowed Hiroshi to ramble, knowing that it mattered little whether this was the same dog. *She was his dog now, and that was enough. But what if this was Uggy Dog, and what of Roni? Why had she abandoned the dog on this planet?*

"Okay dude, that's clean enough." Hiroshi smiled admirably at the well sanded area around the hole. He took epoxy from Hick and smeared it over the cleaned area before applying the patch and smoothing the edges with his palm. "Think it'll work?"

"Of course I do," Hick lied. "Of course I do!" He knew Hiroshi had no more confidence than he did in the patch, but the patch offered a feeling of accomplishment. No longer were they sitting idle. They were finally making progress toward their escape.

At the same time other progress was being made; progress towards the rodeo.

Hick, Hiroshi, and Clint had been given the job of posting fliers. The fliers contained a picture of a munchipod riding a bucking horse. Below the picture was a list of events. Wild Bill's Wild West Show topped the list, followed by robotic calf roping, and bull dogging, while bull riding was at the bottom. This came as an indication to Hick that the threads of their welcome were wearing thin, although Clint reassured them that munchipods weren't nearly as interested in robotics, as they were in "live action;" the kind of live action that only Bubba could provide.

Clint's arms had grown long enough to be useful for small tasks, and rather than hurt his feelings, Hick and Hiroshi allowed him to help post the fliers. Watching Clint served to humor the two men, as he pressed his forehead against a flier to hold it to the wall, while holding the hammer, and attempting to nail it with his underdeveloped arms. Seeing their opportunity, a group of juvenile munchipods snuck up, and pulled Clint's pants down to his ankles. The culprits vanished as quickly as they came, they're high pitched giggles echoing, yet diminishing with their escape.

Hiroshi turned to Hick. "Have you noticed, dude, that munchipods turn bright green when they blush?"

Hick pointed at Clint and chuckled. "I think he needs your help."

"Mister Hiroshi, could you help me please?" Clint pleaded.

"Be right there." Hiroshi laughed as he started toward Clint.

Even Uggy Dog seemed amused.

"Hey little dude, the way your arms are growing, pretty soon you could be a gunslinger again," Hiroshi teased, adding, "seems like they've grown an inch already this morning!"

"Yeah, the sunlight helps a lot. Duke and those kids had better watch out too!" Clint made a punching motion with his tiny right arm.

Hick and Hiroshi had tried to resolve the differences between Clint and Duke but every effort had failed. The only thing that proved successful was to keep them apart.

"Dude, if not for a lack of appendages, they would certainly finish each other off," Hiroshi chuckled, continuing with, "I hope they resolve their differences before their gun arms grow back."

Clint's dexterity seemed to improve with each flyer he posted. Some of his fliers were spaced no more than ten feet apart. He cared little for advertising or workmanship, only the need to prove he could accomplish the task.

Within a few hours Clint's handiwork hung crooked, and sometimes upside down, from one end of town to the next, on every wall and hitching post.

"Well, that's that, Clint!" Hick wanted to convince Clint he was finished.

"You mean we're out of posters?" His expression was one of disappointment.

"No little dude, we're out of walls," Hiroshi said with a tone of sympathy laced with sarcasm.

"Ah, shucky darn!" Clint dropped his head and stared at the boardwalk. "Just when I was gettin' the hang of it."

Hiroshi leaned towards Hick and whispered, "Dude, ya' think that was a pun?"

Hick's attention was torn from Hiroshi by Uggy Dog's low growl. At first he thought she was growling at Clint, but he noticed her senses had honed in on something down the street, perhaps obscured by the buildings or the curvature of the road.

"Easy girl." Hick pulled a wadded leash from his pocket. He unraveled and fastened it to her collar. "Quiet down guys." He motioned to Hiroshi and Clint. They were babbling about whether Clint was truly ambidextrous and how many times his arms had grown back.

"There's something strange goin' on here." Hick pointed down the street.

"Dude, what do you think it is?" Hiroshi strained his eyes.

"Some sort of commotion. Sounded like somebody screaming somewhere near the Livery Stable." Hick allowed Uggy Dog to lead him from the walkway onto the street, keeping tension on the leash. Before he knew it he was running to keep up.

Hiroshi and Clint followed with less enthusiasm.

A group of munchipods had gathered, spreading from one side of the street to the other. The crowd parted slowly to make way for a train of wagons led by a group of green mountain men, armed with bull whips. At the head of the procession, someone, or something crouched huddled under a partially shredded blanket for protection from the lashes. Following the men with whips, Wild Bill drove a buckboard behind a team of robotic mules. At his command the green mountain men unleashed their whips forcing the blanketed form to move forward. The victim released a pitiful cry, the cry of a woman in agony.

Her jerks and groans became weaker with every lash until she could move no more. As the last munchipod spectator stepped aside, Hick and Uggy Dog faced Wild Bill and his cohorts.

Wild Bill pointed his rifle at Hick and scowled, "That's far enough Alien! You crossed me once, don't cross me again!"

The crowd grew silent, so silent Hick could hear Hiroshi and Clint's footsteps, and labored breathing as they came up behind him.

He held Uggy Dog back, wishing he had ten more Rottweiler to turn loose on Wild Bill and his men.

"This is what I'm going to do to you, alien, when the time is right!" Wild Bill pointed to his victim with the barrel of his rifle. He motioned back to Hiroshi and Clint. "And your friend, and his little sidekick as well."

Hick focused on Wild Bill's victim. Bleeding hands with white knuckles clenched tightly over the end of the blanket. Through holes in the fabric, he could see blood streaked, matted brown hair.

"I'll kill you!" Hick shouted, pointing his finger at Wild Bill. Uggy dog lunged at the end of the leash, scattering the whip-men.

Callously, Wild Bill trained the rifle on the victim beneath the blanket.

"Don't do it," Clint said, clutching Hick's pants with his little hands, "He'll kill her!"

Hick stopped cold and pulled Uggy Dog back to his side. Overwhelmed with helplessness, he clenched his teeth together and released a ragged sigh. Perhaps the woman would be better off dead he thought.

"Dude, supress the urge!" Hiroshi's hand gripped Hick's shoulder, "Don't let 'em know you care. They're feeding on your emotion. If you try to save her you could kill her. Her only chance is if you let go."

"You're next, Alien!" Wild Bill released a sadistic laugh. "You're next!" Weasel joined in with his high pitched giggle, and the rest of the mountain men followed with laughter that sounded like a drunken mob on helium.

Hick turned his attention back to Wild Bill's victim. Slowly, painfully, the woman lifted the blanket. Lovely green eyes peered at him from a face stained with blood, dirt and tears. "Hick?" She muttered before collapsing in the dirt.

"Throw her in the wagon, boys," Wild Bill shouted.

Chapter Thirteen

Hiroshi slapped Hick on the back, as the two men entered the crew lounge. "Dude, you did all you could. You can't feel bad about that."

"There's more to it than that." Hick sat down on the couch and leaned forward with his head in his hands. "I feel like I've grown callous. I feel like part of me enjoyed seeing her there. Maybe I didn't act because I wanted her to suffer for leaving me for another guy."

Hiroshi's eyes enlarged, a grin formed on his lips. "Dude, don't tell me that was the girl who jilted you? Are you sure? 'Cause this is getting cornier by the minute. Dude! She'd probably take you back in a hot second now!"

Hick turned his head away, as though stricken with a fowl odor.

"So dude…" Hiroshi seemed to be searching his mind for a topic by which to redeem himself. "What do you think you should have done?"

Hick rolled his eyes, he wasn't ready for the Doctor Hiroshi routine, but the question had its merits. "If I could have got my hands on a laser cannon I'd-a blasted every last one of them little munchkins from here to next Friday and then some. Even the bystanders!"

"Seriously?"

"Seriously," Hick shrugged. "There was nothing I could have done."

"My point exactly!" Hiroshi paused, then his eyes flickered. "Dude, if the dog is here, and the girl is here, then the other guy must be here, too."

Hick offered Hiroshi his *you just figured that out?* expression. "It wouldn't bother me if I saw her boyfriend whipped half dead lying in the street!"

"Dude, let's change the subject and move onto greener pastures. Are the bull riders going to have anything to hang onto this time?"

"Are you kidding? Whose side are you on?"

***

Wild Bill sat at a saloon table surrounded by his men and glared at the huge, hulking woman standing on the stage. "What do you mean they just dropped you off here?" He demanded, continuing with, "You mean they just left without you and abandoned you here?"

Wild Bill's men began to chuckle.

Charlotte waited for silence before speaking, "Yes Wild Bill, that is correct."

Wild Bill raised a beer mug to his lips, tipped, and swallowed. "Now why, do you suppose they did that?" Wild Bill returned the mug to his lips.

Charlotte drew a deep breath, stepped forward, and squinted. "Because they realized that I'm not really one of them! I'm actually one of you!"

Wild Bill began to choke on his beer, while his men erupted with laughter. When he was able to catch his breath he slammed his mug on the table, and demanded, "Silence!" After clearing his throat, he leaned forward. "Do you mean to tell me that you are not really a human, you're one of us?"

"Yes sir, that is exactly what I mean, and I can prove it."

Again laughter filled the room.

"Quiet!" Wild Bill demanded, as he waited for silence. "Charlotte, you are not green, and you are by no means small, so what makes you think you're one of us?"

"Quiet!" Charlotte demanded, with a voice that nearly shook the room. Immediately the laughter ceased and every eye focused on her. "I am a munchipod queen trapped in the body of a woman!"

"Somebody get Charlotte a mirror." Wild Bill shouted above the laughter of his men.

107

"I don't need a mirror," she replied, "get my luggage."

Wild Bill nodded and one of his men carried a suitcase to the edge of the stage. Charlotte stooped and opened the case. She pulled out several packages of virtual goggles and began distributing them throughout the room. "If you'll each put one of these on," She said, "you'll see me for what I really am."

**

"Testing. One, two, three," a voice boomed over the loud speaker high atop the rodeo arena. "Ladies and gentlemen, it is my pleasure to introduce to you the mayor of our fair city, Mayor Ralph."

In the center of the arena, the mayor mounted the podium steps, and took the microphone from one of the councilmen. Scattered applause erupted throughout the grandstands, and died as suddenly as it began.

"Good morning ladies and gentlemen." The mayor waved. "Welcome to the first annual Munchville Stampede. Among the festivities we have planned for your entertainment are two big days of robotic calf roping, bulldogging, barrel racing, and of course bull riding on Mister Hick's real-live western bull."

Thunderous applause rose from the crowd.

"And that's not all." Ralph paused a moment for the applause to subside. "We have a whip exhibition by the one and only, Weasel." The mayor carefully enunciated each word. "And a shooting exhibition by the one, the only, Wild Bill." The crowd applauded heavily. "Following tonight's festivities, mister Hick, and mister Hiroshi are going to teach some real western dancing in the city square, so put on your dancin' shoes and come join us for some high falootin' fun. Now for the robotic calf roping. Bring on the first contestant." The mayor motioned to a group of munchipods waiting inside the main gate. "Boys!" The group gathered around the podium and carried it from the arena with the mayor on top waving to the cheering crowd.

"Ladies and gentlemen." Another voice came over the loud speaker, as the audio was transferred to a booth in the grandstands. "May I direct your attention to the east end of the arena where Dusty Pete is about to make history as the first cowboy on this planet to compete in robotic calf roping."

A gate at the east end of the arena swung open. Out dashed a small robotic calf followed by a little green cowboy swinging a lariat from the back of a robotic horse. Halfway across the arena the cowboy hurled the lariat over the calf's head. He wrapped two loops around the saddle horn, and brought the horse to an abrupt skid, jerking the calf backward to the ground. The cowboy dismounted and after tying the calf's legs, threw his hands in the air. The crowd went wild, releasing wolf whistles and cheers.

"Wasn't that spectacular folks?" the loud speaker blared. "That was Dusty Pete with an official time of six point five seconds. Let's hear it for Dusty Pete." Pete bowed, hat in hand, first to one side of the grandstands then to the other.

After untying the calf, a couple of cowboys herded it from the arena.

"Our next contestant is...

***

Hick and Hiroshi, along with Uggy Dog, approached the carnival booth, and pens, where the bull and cows were kept. They could hear the loud speaker in the distance although they paid little attention.

"How much do you know about rocket fuel, Hiroshi?" Hick patted Uggy Dog's head.

"Dude, there's multiple possibilities. The ship is capable of converting, and running on a number of different substances, agena, UDMH, Liquid Hydrogen, and multiple types of Hydrazine, or Kerosene. If we can get anything close, the ship's computer will automatically adjust the engines to accommodate the fuel mixture."

"I'll talk to Clint to see if he can come up with something. He probably won't know first hand, but he might know who to ask."

"Up-turn all the stones, dude," Hiroshi's words lacked enthusiasm.

Hick knew Clint would have no answer to the fuel problem, and asking was little more than a lost cause, but escape was foremost on his mind, and if it meant searching every avenue, he would.

"What is all this?" Hick pointed to several rows of boxes and crates in front of the carnival booth. The boxes ranged from small to huge, stacked neatly in rows over a fifty square foot area. "This wasn't here yesterday was it?"

"No."

The two men started down the rows of boxes.

An eight foot wooden wheel, mounted upright on a steel pedestal caught Hick's eye. Affixed to it were straps with buckles for fastening someone or something. The wheel turned freely when Hick touched it. He moved down the row to a crate nine feet tall, and equally wide, covered with canvas. Pulling back a corner of the canvas, he discovered a barred cage beneath. Squinting, he peered through the bars into the darkness, but saw nothing. He pulled the canvas back farther. His eyes found a slim feminine figure crouched in the shadows. "Roni, is that you?" He pulled on the bars, testing their strength and found them secure.

"Hick, I don't want you to see me like this," she sobbed.

"Why are you hiding? Did you know it was me?"

"Yes, I heard you talking." She stepped further into the shadows.

Uggy dog moved close to the cage, whining and wagging an impatient greeting.

"Why didn't you say something? Why don't you want to see me?"

"I don't think there's much hope for me, Hick. There's nothing you can do. The cage is foolproof, and Wild Bill is very dangerous. I don't want you to get hurt or killed. I just want you to remember me the way I was when..." Her words gave way to sobbing.

"When what? I need you to finish."

"What'd you find, dude?" Hiroshi rounded the end of the row.

"Stay away." Hick held up a cautioning hand.

Hiroshi nodded. Turning, he disappeared around the end of the row.

"When what?" Hick repeated softly.

"When we made love," she sobbed.

"I still love you," Hick heard himself say. "No matter what happens, I want you to know that."

"I'll always love you too. I realize you are the only man I have ever loved."

"What about the guy you ran off with? You didn't love him?" There was a hint of sarcasm in his voice.

"I didn't run off with Bo. He kidnapped me at gunpoint. He said he would kill you if I didn't go."

Hick paused to think for a long moment. Pain filled his sinuses and moisture formed in his eyes. He sensed she was telling the truth. Why would she lie to him now? Slipping beneath the canvas, he moved from bar to bar, tugging, but found no weakness. The cage door was solid with three locks and latches; top, center and bottom. "Don't worry," he said, trying to sound calm, "I'll find a way to get you out of here. I don't know when or how, but I'll find a way."

Roni moved closer. Her face was thin and pale. Her eyes lacked the old luster. She nodded and sniffled, wiping her face on the sleeve of a ragged robe. Reaching through the bars, she patted Uggy Dog. "Oh Lucki." She forced an agonizing smile and held it briefly between sobs, "I'm glad you're all right."

We'll be back for you!" Hick breathed a sigh of relief, knowing he had brought Roni a moment of happiness.

"Hey, dude. If you're finished there, come over here, I got something I want you to see," Hiroshi's voice carried over the row of boxes.

As Hick approached he heard a familiar voice snarl, "Shut up ya little twerp. Let go of the canvas and leave me alone. If I weren't behind these bars I'd teach you some manners."

Uggy Dog rushed towards the bars growling. The man stepped back slightly.

"Dude, you talk tough behind the safety of those bars." Hiroshi chuckled before turning to Hick, "Hey Hick. Is this the cowardly dude that held a gun on you, and hit you from behind?"

"Hmmm, can't say for sure," Hick rubbed his chin and glared. "The guy was ugly and stupid, but I'm not sure he was that ugly or stupid."

"You ain't seen ugly friend," Bo growled. "Ugly is what I'm going to do to you when I get out of here."

"I think you're right, dude." Hiroshi winked at Hick, "They probably penned him up to keep people from catching the stupid virus."

Sincerity filled Hick's eyes as he glared at Bo. "I hope you do get out. I'm gonna make you wish you were back in there." Nodding to Hiroshi, he said, "Come on, let's get out of here."

As the two men walked away, Bo continued pelting them with insults and profanity.

Turning, Hiroshi blurted, "Dude, that cage isn't getting any bigger, and you're gonna' bullshit yourself into a corner." The suggestion did little to quiet Bo, but it gave Hick and Hiroshi a moment of laughter and the feeling that they had gained the advantage over the ranting of a madman.

***

At the cattle pens Hick fed the cows, allowing Bubba only a small portion before snapping the lead rope to his nose. "C'mon Bubba." He tugged gently. The bull showed reluctance at first, but followed on the second tug.

Hiroshi waited for Hick to exit with the bull before closing and locking the pen.

Sunlight filtered through openings beneath the roof and around the pens and stalls, illuminating airborne dust particles that hovered above the sawdust floor. Sounds from the rodeo grew louder, as the two men, along with the bull and dog, made their way down the corridor towards the arena.

"How about that folks," the loud speaker blared, "Another record! Cowboy Ron has just set the fourth record of the day in the calf roping competition with a time of five-point seven seconds. Let's hear it for Cowboy Ron."

The crowd responded with moderate applause mingled with a few boos and hisses.

Hick glanced back and chuckled at Hiroshi who walked several paces behind the bull. He wondered if he would do the same if a flying hoof had narrowly missed his head in the last rodeo.

Hiroshi's eyes seemed to light up and his mouth enlarged with a grin. "Just think, dude, I came here a lowly spaceship driver, and look at me now, I've been a rodeo clown, cattle drover, and a spokesman for one of the planet's greatest exhibits. Dude, I could go back home and run for office, dude! I could be the Governor of California. Dude! With those qualifications I could be President!"

Hick half turned and nodded. Uggy Dog seemed to be smiling from behind Hiroshi's leg.

After placing the bull in the rodeo chute, the two men perched atop the stall to watch the bulldogging, while Uggy Dog sat behind the fence outside the chute watching the action through the boards .

"Where's Clint?" Hick scanned both grandstands, caring little about Clint's whereabouts, hoping to take his mind off Roni.

"I don't know." Hiroshi glanced around and shrugged. "I haven't seen him all day."

"He'll probably be along soon." Hick heard his voice drop slightly. He hoped Hiroshi hadn't noticed his sadness.

"Dude," Hiroshi replied, "I know he wanted to see this."

***

"And now, Ladies and Gentlemen, it's time for the bulldogging competition," the loud speaker boomed. "First off, is Rustlin' Roy."

"YeeeeeeeeeeHaaaaaaaa," came a loud squeal from a wiry green cowboy atop his robotic horse in the bulldogging chute. He waved his hat to the crowd and smiled.

The announcer continued, "Yes sir folks, for those of you who didn't know it, that's Rustlin' Roy!"

Two chutes opened; from one dashed a robotic steer. From the other, Rustlin' Roy on a robotic steed, his hat in one hand, reins in the other. Roy stood in the stirrups leaning into every lurch. His body appeared motionless amid the rapid movement of the horse. Coming abreast of the steer, Roy donned the hat. With another loud "YeeeeeeeeHaaaaaaaaa," he flung himself from the horse to a position just behind the steer's head. Skidding, bridging, and twisting, he brought the steer to the ground with a thud in a cloud of dust.

"Dude, did you see that?" Hiroshi eyes seemed to bulge. He clutched the board beneath him to maintain his balance.

"Yeah, I can't believe these little guys!" Hick shouted, competing with the thunderous applause.

"Let's hear it for Rustlin' Roy," the loud speakers blared.

Chapter Fourteen

"Draw Duke," Clint challenged, standing in front of a dresser mirror in his hotel room, his hat tilted over one eye. He cocked his head, forcing the slightest hint of insincerity from his face. His fingers quivered over two six guns slung low on his hips. He raised a threatening eyebrow. "You talkin' ta' me, Duke?" That would never do! He straightened making his look more menacing, his voice lower. "You talkin' ta' may? His hands jerked, his eyes enlarged, he turned suddenly. "All right, make my day! Try ta' pull my pants down again, and I'll blast ya' from here ta' next Friday," he growled, drawing both revolvers with lightning precision. "Gotcha." He spun his guns back into the holsters. "Oh no, I almost forgot, they're waiting for me!" Rushing from the room, he slammed the door behind him.

The carnival booth seemed abandoned when Clint arrived. An occasional announcement, or cheering from the distant arena, the only sounds.

The rows of boxes caught Clint's attention. He decided to investigate. Tiptoeing cautiously, he made his way down the first row. Startled by a movement, he turned and drew. He found himself facing his own reflection in one of two side-by-side mirrors. In one mirror Clint appeared short and fat, while the other made him tall and slim. Twirling and spinning the pistols in and out of his holsters, he repeated, "ya' just have ta ask yourself one question, Duke. Do I feel lucky? Well, do ya', Duke?" He used a low, slow voice in front of his tall image and a high pitched rapid voice for the shorter, following each demonstration with a chuckle.

The sound of approaching voices caught his attention. "All right Duke," he whispered, throwing himself behind one of the crates. His fingers twitched in nervous anticipation as he peered cautiously around the corner of the crate. It wasn't

Duke. Clint breathed a disappointed sigh. It was Wild Bill and Weasel. They were speaking to a burly human in a cage.

"I've got information that will help you," the man boasted.

Clint leaned as close to the corner of the crate as he could without being seen, straining his ears to hear every word.

"All I want is my freedom and their spaceship. I want your word on it."

"All right, you've got it." Wild Bill nodded. "Tell me what you know."

"The woman." The burley man pointed. "She's Hick's woman. You can get to him by using her."

Wild Bill thought for a moment. "I know just what I'll do." He raised his right hand in a fist and shook it. "First we'll challenge him to fight you, Boo." He turned to Weasel and smiled. Turning back to Bo, he continued, "after all, you're bigger than he is, and I heard you say you could whip him."

A look of discontent fell across Bo's face. He replaced it with a confident grin. "Piece-a-cake. I whipped him once before. The man's a wimp!"

Wild Bill pointed at Roni's cage with a cunning grin. "After the fight tomorrow, I'll put a bullet between her eyes while that alien watches. I'm sick of having her around anyway. She can't sing and all she does is eat. Besides, now that we got Charlotte, we don't need her anymore."

"Whoa!" Turning, Clint crept away.

***

The excitement of the rodeo and the creative ability of the munchipods had taken Hick's mind off Roni. *If they could imagine it, they could do it.* It was obvious by the way they had fashioned their culture. It was evidenced by the robotic animals they built; horses, steers, calves. It was true in the way they built the arena with its grandstands, stock pens, chutes and corrals, and now it had been proven in the way they rode, roped and bulldogged.

"Dude, isn't that Clint over there?" Hiroshi pointed to a munchipod, making his way across the opposite grandstands.

"Sure looks like him." Hick squinted, raising his hand over his brow to shield the sunlight. "I expected him to come from the other direction."

"Dude, it's so Clint to come the hard way," Hiroshi said with a smirk, adding, "The little dude's totin' guns again." .

Clint made his way to the end of the grandstands, climbing under the railing and over fences. Reaching the chute out of breath, he glared as though uncertain where to begin.

"Dude, you look like you've seen a ghost." Hiroshi grinned.

"What happened?" Hick held back a laugh. "Did you run into Duke on the way over here?"

"Listen carefully." Clint stepped closer. paying little attention to the kidding. Between labored breaths he forced, "I overheard Wild Bill, and Weasel, and that alien, talking."

Hick felt the smile leave his face.

"They're gonna' kill her tomorrow! Boo told 'em she's your woman. Wild Bill is going to challenge you to fight Boo and after Boo wins, Wild Bill's gonna kill the alien woman and give Boo your ship. He said he doesn't need her anymore 'cause he's got something called Charlotte."

"Charlotte?" The two men repeated in unison, looking at one another.

What, kill her after Boo…You mean if Bo wins?" Hick felt blood rush to his head. "Bo's not gonna' win, and we're not gonna' let Wild Bill kill her."

"Dude, stop the clock." Hiroshi motioned for Hick's attention. "We gotta' have a plan first. You can't just go and break her out."

"Yeah," Clint added, "that's stealin', they'd hang you for sure!"

117

"Dude, if we had rocket fuel and knew for certain we could make a quick getaway." Hiroshi looked Hick in the eye. He seemed to be waiting for some kind of acknowledgment.

"Do you know where we could get rocket fuel, Clint?" Hick heard himself say.

"Rocket fuel? Never heard of it."

"We can still take off on auxiliary fuel, can't we, Hiroshi?" Hick words were desperate, almost panicky.

"Maybe dude, but we need to know for sure. As it stands, dude, I'm not certain we could make it out of the atmosphere. We've been using what we have to run the generator and power the batteries."

"What are we gonna' do?" Hick felt his strength escaping.

"Not to worry, dude, we'll think of something." Hiroshi's tone was filled with false confidence. "But right now we gotta get the bull ready!"

***

"And now for the event you've all been waiting for; the bull riding competition!"

Tumultuous applause rose from the crowd.

Hick tried to summon his faculties. He swung his legs over the fence and dropped to the ground. "Move, Uggy Dog," he demanded.

Sensing Hick's mood, Uggy Dog quickly backed away.

Hick grabbed the flank rope from the fence and motioned to Hiroshi on the opposite side.

Reaching under the boards, Hick flung the end of the rope under the bull to Hiroshi. Together they walked the ends upward to the top of Bubba's back. Hick joined the rope in a half hitch. Bubba began to step nervously as Hick pulled it tighter than usual. Turning, Hick nodded and motioned for the rider.

A munchipod cowboy climbed the chute gate. He stopped at the top and looked at Bubba with fear in his eyes.

"The first rider is Wiley," the announcer declared.

"That's Willy," the rider corrected with a trembling voice.

"What's that?" the announcer returned, unable to hear over the chatter of the crowd.

"He says his name's Willy!" people in the stands relayed the message.

"The name is Willy, undertaker take note," the announcer corrected.

Willy positioned himself uneasily on the back of the restless bull.

Hick nodded and raised his arm. A hush fell over the crowd. "Let 'er go," he shouted, dropping his arm. The chute gate flew open. Out lunged the bull with Willy on his back. Bubba's first kick threw Willy ten feet up and over the fence. He landed on his feet in the empty chute. Hick leaped from the fence and ran after Bubba. The bull swung violently and kicked, just missing Hick's face with his back hooves. Hick grabbed the flank rope and loosened it with a tug.

"Did you see that folks, how lucky can you get?" the announcer asked.

The crowd rose to their feet with a chorus of "ooos" and "awes".

A team of munchipod rodeo clowns jumped from positions along the fence and herded Bubba from the arena.

Hick flung the flank rope over the top of the fence, where Hiroshi sat bursting with laughter, and climbed up to join him. "I'm with you." He breathed a sigh of relief. "Where do we get the popcorn? Might as well let the rodeo clowns do their job, right?"

Hiroshi released a chuckle and shook his head. "Dude, it's good to see you lighten up a little."

The small clowns herded, and baited the restless bull down a narrow sawdust passageway and back to the chute.

119

They helped Hick and Hiroshi slide the retaining boards in place and flank Bubba.

"You guys are on your own. I'm not going out there." Hick motioned for the next rider.

"We're gonna' use barrels this time," one of the clowns commented, as he climbed down from the chute.

Hick followed the clowns with his eyes across the arena where three wooden barrels lined the fence.

"Our next rider is, Jay Strongarrow," the announcer declared.

A munchipod in a red flannel shirt, and crumpled black cowboy hat, with a feather protruding from the top, crossed the corner of the arena. He seemed emotionless as he climbed the fence and mounted Bubba.

Seeing the bull agitated bothered Hick. He swore this would be the last rodeo he would commit Bubba to.

When the barrels were in place he raised his arm and dropped it. The chute gate opened. Out charged the bull twirling and spinning, left, then right. The sudden change in direction caught Jay off guard, he fell to the ground landing on his back. Bubba turned and charged striking Jay with the impact of a locomotive, smashing him into the fence and goring him violently.

One upward parry of the horns sent an arm, a leg, and a cowboy hat hurtling upward. The crowd was aghast. Immediately one of the clowns rushed in and released the rope from the bull's flank, then rushed back to join the others. The clowns began taunting the bull. Bubba turned from his dismembered quarry to face the three clowns positioned at equal intervals approximately thirty feet away. He charged the one in the middle.

The little clown ran and dove into a barrel, narrowly escaping the slashing horns. Turning, Bubba went for the second clown, who, panic stricken, ran toward the third. Together they attempted to elude the bull by diving into the same barrel where the first hid. The crowd screamed, as the third clown's legs scissor kicked above the barrel, before sliding in.

"Dude, it's like this was rehearsed, and even Bubba knows his cue," Hiroshi shouted as he watched the bull throw the barrel around the arena. The barrel splintered and the three clowns, exposed, scattered and ran, each scaling the fence with the bull in close pursuit. Two munchipod cowboys jumped from the fence outside the coral and closed the gate.

"Nothing surprises me anymore!" Hick called back, competing with the roar of the crowd.

Jay's feather fluttered downward through the air in front of the grandstands. A stretcher crew rushed in to gather what was left of the little green Indian. As they carried him away, he pointed with his remaining hand to his severed arm and leg. The stretcher crew stopped to gather each of the limbs before exiting the arena.

Hick turned and noticed Clint under the grandstands gathering money which was falling from the shocked audience.

"Our next rider is...." The announcer stopped short when he noticed the contestants on the fence shaking their heads. "Well, I guess we don't have any more riders, so without further adieu, we'll continue with Wild Bill's Wild West Show."

Mild applause rose from the awestricken crowd.

"Next we have the one and only, Weasel, with a bullwhip exhibition."

A group of eight munchipods rolled a large wheel and platform, in wheelbarrow fashion, through the gate at the west end of the arena. Six of them held the platform on which the wheel sat, while two steadied the wheel. They set the wheel and platform upright near the center of the arena, and tested it to make sure it turned freely. Hick recognized the wheel from the rows of boxes near the carnival booth, and wondered what purpose it could possibly serve. Certainly nothing good, he told himself.

Roni was led into the arena, her hands tied and a blindfold over her eyes. She wore a buckskin dress and moccasins. Her hair hung behind her in a single braid. Two munchipods, dressed in buckskins led her on a leash attached to a collar around her neck. They guided her up a small portable step to the wheel, where they strapped her wrists and ankles.

When she was securely fastened, they removed her moccasins, and placed what appeared to be straws between her fingers, toes and lips. One of the munchipods removed the portable step, while the other climbed the side of the wheel to set it in motion. After jumping off the wheel, the munchipod tugged on it until it spun rapidly.

Weasel entered the arena from the east and walked slowly towards Roni. He stopped in front of the wheel where he turned and bowed low in an arrogant fashion. The crowd responded with moderate applause. Turning back to the wheel, Weasel raised the whip and released the coil. Five cracks rang out in succession as the straws flew from Roni's toes, hands and lips. He drew the whip back like a yoyo and blew a kiss to the crowd, bowing once again to tumultuous praise. When the applause died he cast a spiteful glance at Hick and Hiroshi, and strode back across the arena making his exit through the same gate from which he'd entered.

"Ladies and gentlemen, it's time for the final event of today's rodeo. Don't forget the dance tonight in the town square, and more rodeo action tomorrow. Now will you please welcome Wild Bill." The crowd responded with healthy applause as Wild Bill entered the arena from the same gate Weasel exited. He wore a fine buckskin outfit with a holster and two six guns. He carried his buffalo rifle cradled across his chest. Two helpers followed, each carrying a hammer and nails, and what appeared to be an arm load of ceramic disks. Wild Bill stopped about thirty yards from the spinning wheel while the two helpers continued. After catching the wheel and bringing it to a stop, they nailed the ceramic discs, twelve in all, around Roni's body.

"Clint, Clint." Hick felt his heart racing. "You're positive he's not planning to kill her till tomorrow?"

"That's what he said. He won't want the audience to think he could miss, so I'm sure he'll announce it before he kills her."

"Dude, you're shit'n me!" The color was gone from Hiroshi's face. "He can't purposely kill her in front of all these people, can he?"

Clint shrugged and squinted. "To us, uh, I mean to them." Clint pointed at the crowd. "She's an alien slave. She has no rights. This crowd will pay a lot to see her die." He gestured with his right arm towards the grandstands, and paused to admire the arm. "Will ya' look at that? That's a pretty nice arm, isn't it?"

Hick rubbed his forehead with disgust.

Wild Bill's two helpers banded a lock of Roni's hair, and nailed it to the wheel just above her head.

Wild Bill examined the cartridge in his rifle and closed the breach. He nodded to the two munchipods. They took turns tugging downward on the wheel until a second nod from Wild Bill told them it was fast enough.

One of the helpers brought the portable step to Wild Bill before leaving the arena. Wild Bill leaned the rifle against the step while he checked the cylinders of his six guns. After closing the cylinders, he twirled them rapidly before slipping them back into the holsters. He looked into the grandstands and nodded to the announcer.

"Ladies and gentlemen. You're attention please."

The crowd grew silent.

"This next trick requires a great deal of concentration, so we ask that you remain in your seats and keep silent. Wild Bill will attempt to shoot twelve ceramic discs from around the alien on the wheel using his six shooters, and then with his rifle he will shoot a lock from her hair. I would like to caution you at this time; do not try this at home."

Wild Bill bowed low, facing the wheel with arms outstretched towards the grandstands. Straightening, he turned and cast Hick a sadistic smile.

Hick glared back, trying to maintain his composure. He realized his hands were quivering and he hoped Wild Bill hadn't noticed.

Wild Bill fixed his attention on Roni. With lightning speed he drew the revolvers. Twelve shots rang out rapidly, as he shook the pistols from his hip, as though they were Mexican gourds. Ceramic fragments flew from the wheel, as each slug found it's mark. After the last shot, he twirled the pistols back into his holsters.

"Those must be double action revolvers," Clint observed.

Hick turned to hear what Clint was saying.

"You know I could do that!" He shook his hands in the same fashion as Wild Bill.

Hick turned back to the arena in fear and distaste, just as Wild Bill wetted the sight and leveled his rifle.

"Shut up little dude!" Hiroshi whispered through clenched teeth.

Clint stood with hands outstretched, a look of bewilderment on his face.

Wild Bill raised the rifle and took aim but hesitated. He lowered the rifle to his hip, as though he had changed his mind. A loud boom rang out, as a cloud of smoke expanded around him.

Hick clenched his eyes shut. A chill gripped him, and traveled down his spine. When he forced his eyes open the wheel was slowing. Hair and pieces of Roni's headband filled the air and fluttered to the ground around her. She was alive! He released a sigh of relief. He hadn't fully realized how much she meant to him or what life would be like without her.

"How about that, Ladies, and gentlemen? Wasn't that spectacular?" Wild Bill wants to invite you all back tomorrow to see him place the last slug directly between the Alien woman's eyes."

Excitement rose from the crowd in the form of oos and awes, as they filtered from the crowded grandstands.

Chapter Fifteen

"Where do you want this?" Clint held up a portable stereo.

"Just put it over there." Hick pointed to one of the hay bales bordering the dance area. "Are the batteries up in that thing?"

Dusk was coming on fast and Hick was tense. He patted Uggy Dog, and pushed her away with his knee. "Go lay down somewhere and leave me alone." He felt like saying the same to the group of twenty munchipods working to set up the dance, but they needed him for instructions, and he needed to keep busy for his sanity.

Clint set the stereo on a bale next to one of the lanterns and switched it on. The words "John Deere Green" blared out.

"Shut that thing off!" Hick heard himself shout.

The workers froze.

Clint switched the stereo off. "Sorry."

"Go on with your work," Hick said in a relenting voice.

Hiroshi entered the lighted area inside the bales. He gripped Hick's arm and whispered, "Dude, you gotta' get a hold of yourself. This is a special occasion for these little dudes, and whether or not you share in the spirit, you have to keep your head on straight, 'cause, dude, we need all the friends we can get."

"You're right." Hick scratched his forehead nervously and nodded, "I'll try to keep it under control."

Hiroshi slapped Hick on the arm and smiled. "Dude, We'll break her out tonight." Turning to Clint, Hiroshi shouted, "Dude, commence with the festivities!"

Clint reached for the *on* switch then hesitated waiting for Hick's approval.

Hick forced a smile and nodded.

Clint switched the stereo on and returned the smile.

"Yeeeee Haaaaaa dude," Hiroshi howled clapping and stomping off beat, as the music began. *"We're gonna dance,"* by Lavender Blue.

Grabbing two chubby munchipod women, one on either side, Hiroshi began to dance. The little women tried to imitate his every turn, step, and clap.

"Not like that, Hiroshi," Hick wanted to shout, as he buried his face in his hands and emerged laughing uncontrollably.

"C'mon dude, I need some help here," Hiroshi called out with a tone that was half scolding half suggesting.

Hick nodded and ordered Uggy dog to lie down and stay, emphasizing the command with a shake of his index finger. He entered the dance area, falling in beside one of the munchipod ladies. "Back right, left, right and stomp," he repeated under his breath. "Hip rocks and hold, quarter turn, stomp and half turn, right vine and stomp-clap." Hiroshi tried to follow Hick, leaving the munchipod women a complete step behind. The dance area filled quickly, as hundreds of munchipods joined in formation, clapping, swaying, stomping and turning.

Lost in the moment, Hick watched the crowd follow his every step. *If they could only see this back on earth! Na, on second thought, as soon as this ended he would deny it ever happened.*

By the fifth song the munchipods had caught on to the dance steps, and Hick decided to sit out. He allowed Uggy dog to lay her head on his lap, as he sat on a bale patting her gently.

"Dude, there must be three hundred of them out there, and a couple hundred more waiting for a turn." Hiroshi wiped sweat from his forehead, as he sat down on a bale opposite Uggy Dog. "How goes it, Galactic Mutt?"

"I think they've got the hang of it." Hick nodded to the dancing crowd.

"Dude!" Hiroshi nodded and waved to the crowd, "they picked up those dance steps a lot quicker than we did."

After the song the group faced Hick and Hiroshi, offering a round of applause and laughter. The two men waved and nodded graciously.

Realizing the music had ended, Clint abandoned his partner, a little green bar maid, and pressed through the crowd to the stereo. He dug impatiently through a box containing disks. Taking a disk at random, he inserted it and adjusted the volume. The sound of steel guitars rang out followed by the voice of Elvis, *"since my baby left me..."*

Hick noticed Hiroshi's head, arm, and leg begin to move in perfect rhythm to the beat. As though compelled by a strange force, Hiroshi jerked to his feet. His head and hands went limp while his right knee gyrated.

Twice Hick reached for Hiroshi, trying to gain his attention, but to no avail.

The baffled crowd made room for Hiroshi and watched in astonishment as his dance posture evolved from a pigeon toed, knock kneed trudge, to an all out pelvic twist. The song continued.

"I'm so lonely baby, oh I'm so lonely..."

At first Hick felt embarrassed, then he noticed the munchipods imitating Hiroshi's movements, swinging their knees, and shoulders, freezing at every syncopated rest.

"I'm so lonely, I could die."

At the end of the song, Hiroshi returned to the bale exhausted, perspiration beading on his forehead. "Dude, it's humid out here, isn't it? Where's the little dude? When is he going to start that music?"

Hick nodded and shrugged, searching his mind for the right response. "You know how Clint is. He'll get around to it."

As the next song began, Hick turned to watch the Munchipods perform a fast gyration to the slow beat of Elvis', *"I can't help falling in love with you."*

"Dude, they're developing their own dance-style. It's got an Elvis-look to it." Hiroshi pulled a straw from the bale and lit it in the lantern. "Dude, you never know what's going to happen next."

"Whoa." A munchipod driver laid back on the reins, bringing his cargo wagon to a stop behind the two men. He wrapped the reins around the brake handle, lifted his hat, and scratched his balding green head. "Who ordered the rot gut?"

A crowd formed around the wagon exchanging munchipod dollars for bottles of rot gut, as fast as the driver could pass them out.

The rot gut had an almost immediate effect on the munchipods, causing them to stagger and slur their words.

A portion of the crowd returned to the dance area, stumbling and falling over one another. One of the munchipods tripped over Hiroshi's foot and dropped his bottle. Somersaulting over a bale, he came to rest unconscious behind them. Hick reached for the bottle, as the intoxicant oozed into a puddle on the ground

"Smells kinda like kerosene. Doesn't it?"

"More like JP-5 with a touch of ether." Hiroshi watched the intoxicated crowd with fascination. When the flame reached his fingers, he dropped the straw and jumped to his feet.

The spilled fluid burst into a fireball. Hick dropped the bottle, which ignited, flying upward with a sizzling noise. The bottle exploded in the sky above, sprinkling every color of the rainbow upon the night darkness.

Silence fell over the crowd, as they watched the fiery particles blossom, and sprinkle evenly in the sky above.

Lighting their empty bottles in like manner, the drunken munchipods sent one after another hissing upward, bursting into a colored array against the blackened canopy. Uggy Dog rushed for cover under the wagon.

Hiroshi turned to the wagon driver. "Dude, how much of this stuff can you get?"

"How much do you want and how soon do you need it?"

"About five thousand gallons, dude, and right now!"

The driver squinted and scratched his ear. "Well let me see, that's a mighty tall order. Cost ya' about five thousand dollars."

"Do you take check or money order?" Hick chuckled, but ceased abruptly when no one joined him.

"Dude, we'll deliver the money. You deliver the rot gut to our ship." Hiroshi glanced over his shoulder. "Little dude! Where's the little dude?"

"I'll find him for you." A chubby munchipod women batted a pair of adoring eyes at Hiroshi.

The smile faded from Hiroshi's face. "Okay, why don't you do that," he blurted with words half stuttered.

The woman giggled and batted again. Turning, she disappeared into the crowd. Moments later Clint staggered to the wagon with a half empty bottle. "Here I am, big dude," he said with a hiccup.

"Go with this driver, little dude, and show him where the ship is." Hiroshi snatched the bottle from Clint and gave it a toss. "We've got other business to attend to, but we'll meet you there shortly." He turned to Hick. "Dude, I got a hacksaw and some wire for picking locks. Let's see if we can break her out."

The two men hurried down the poorly lit street with Uggy Dog following.

When they reached the carnival exhibit they rushed to Roni's cage.

Drawing back the canvas, Hick whispered, "Roni, Roni."

Uggy Dog began to growl.

"Looking for someone?" Weasel stepped from the shadows within the cage and peered through the bars. "She's not here! Of course maybe I can take a message. How should we begin?" He raised a crooked green index finger. "How about, my dearest Veronica. It pains me so not being able to see you on this, the eve of your death, but I'll blow you a kiss from my seat along the arena fence, as Wild Bill blows your brains out." Weasel's lips twisted into a smile revealing green teeth filled with dark cavities .

"Poor Hick, always the loser," came Bo's voice from the other cage. "A loser at love and now a looser at life. You never could understand that nice guys finish last. By the way, she owed me big time for all the lawsuits she caused when she left the concert tour. Since I had to leave Earth to keep from losing everything, I decided to take her with me. Your woman? She was good, she paid her dues, but I don't have a use for her anymore. In fact you can have her back." He followed with a miserable low pitched laugh.

Weasel joined with a sinister soprano giggle. "I've got a message for you." He chuckled viciously. "If you want your woman back, be ready to trade the bull for her during the rodeo tomorrow." He began to laugh again, as he pushed the cage door open and stepped out. "Now if you'll excuse me gentlemen, I've got things to do and people to see." His laugh faded as he walked down the sawdust corridor and disappeared into the darkness.

Hick snapped his fingers and pointed. Uggy Dog raced into the darkness after Weasel. The high pitched laugh turned to shrieks, half drowned by the dog's snarls and growls. The shrieks grew fainter and more helpless as the dog's savagery increased.

"Dude, I knew sooner or later you'd snap!" Hiroshi said, trying unsuccessfully to hold back laughter. "Dude, don't ya' get it, Snapped?" He snapped his fingers. His face sobered. "Oh, never mind!"

Placing two fingers to his lips, Hick whistled. The snarling stopped, and Uggy Dog returned. She stood in front of Hick, wagging. Green slobber oozed from her mouth. She sneezed vigorously, rubbing her mouth against her paws in order to rid herself of the taste. To Hick her expression resembled a smile.

"You haven't heard the last of me, Alien!" Weasel's faint voice came from the corridor.

Once again Hick snapped his fingers. The dog rushed back into the darkness, snarling and growling.

"No, no, please call her off."

Hick whistled again and Uggy Dog returned to his side.

Stepping over to Bo's cage, Hick pulled back the canvas and glared into Bo's dark eyes. "Nice guys may finish last, but you won't finish at all!" He raised his index finger. "I'll personally see to that!" With a smile he released the canvas and allowed it to fall back into place.

Hiroshi lifted the canvas, and added, "Dude, you gotta' ease off on the hotthinkyar."

"What's that supposed to mean?" Bo growled.

"Dude, that's when you're not as hot as you think ya' are." Dropping the canvas, Hiroshi followed Hick, while Bo shouted mindless profanities behind them.

Sub Chapter 15A

From a restaurant table two floors above the Munchville streets, Charlotte peered out the window and watched the fireworks lighting the dark green sky. She longed for something, anything—to take her mind off Wild Bill, seated across the table, watching her through virtual goggles, his spellbound gaze fastened upon her.

"Have I told you how beautiful you are?" he said.

"Only six times tonight," she replied, continuing with, "So what's the occasion?"

"Whatever do you mean, my darling?"

"I mean the fireworks." She pointed out the window.

"That's what happens when cowboys take to drinking and have a good time." He reached across the table and clasped her huge, hulking hand. "But tonight is about us. Let's just shut the rest of the world out." With his free hand he raised his glass and nodded.

Taking her glass, Charlotte raised, and touched it to Wild Bill's, she tipped and swallowed. "Ugh," she grunted, holding the glass back from her lips, as she peered at the bright yellow fluid inside.

"My dear, you've hardly touched your food," said Wild Bill, you make me feel as though I'm eating alone."

Charlotte took a bite, chewed, and swallowed. "You say this is a delicacy?"

"Yes," said Wild Bill, "Some call it Manna, they say it's been known to fall from the sky, others just call it Galactic Bull Pie."

"Hmm, interesting," Charlotte replied, taking another bite.

***

The walk back to the ship was more tedious than the earlier jaunt to Roni's cage. Not because of the two cows, which Hick and Hiroshi led, but because hopes of recovering Roni were all but dashed.

Hick broke the silence. "I'll trade the bull, in fact I'd give anything." "Both cows are bred and hopefully one of them will give birth to a bull calf."

"Dude, don't trust Wild Bill, 'cause I don't." Hiroshi's cow lagged stubbornly. He wrapped the lead rope around his waist and walked backwards. "I wouldn't be surprised if he plans to kill Roni after he gets the bull."

"I don't trust him." Hick shook his head. "I wonder what Bo meant by "law suits from a concert tour?"

"Dude? Oh, you mean that big dude in the cage? I heard him say that too. She does look a lot like that famous pop star, Veronica, who left a concert tour and never came back. Dude, I bought a ticket to see her. I was highly ticked when she didn't show. I wonder if your Roni could be Veronica."

"Pop star? Veronica?"

"Dude, you never heard of Veronica?"

"I'm not really into all that stuff."

"You gotta be kiddin'. She was the hottest thing since ice cream candy bars." Hiroshi glanced at Hick's face. His smile melted. "Dude, how do I get this cow to walk faster?"

"Huh? Oh, you're doing just fine."

*

Two moons had risen and set by the time Hick and Hiroshi reached the ship. Five wagons loaded with rot gut waited for them. The five drivers stood in a circle talking by the lead wagon while Clint sat with his back against the front wheel holding his head with both hands and moaning.

"Here they come now." One of the drivers pointed. "Here's your payload Mister, where's the pay?"

"Dude, I'll get it for you." Hiroshi handed Hick the lead rope while he entered the combination and waited for the

134

hatch to open. "Meanwhile, if you little dudes will help fuel this ship I'll give you a bonus," he called back to the drivers.

"How much of a bonus?"

"Fifty dollars apiece?" Hiroshi beamed with a tone that reminded Hick of the "Step right up," carnival sales-pitch.

"Mister, you got yourself a deal."

The drivers formed a line, tossing the bottles hand to hand from the wagons to the top of a stepladder, where the first driver emptied them into the fuel tank. Once the bottles were emptied he tossed them to the ground where they broke.

"Aren't these recyclable?" Hick pointed to the pile of broken glass.

"Hell no," the first driver replied, "what are you gonna' do with a pile of broken glass?"

"No I mean recycle the bottles." Hick wished he hadn't brought it up.

"You mean, save the bottles?" The second driver's movements slowed, distracted by Hick's suggestion.

"Save the bottles!" A third scratched his head and squinted. "Why then we couldn't break 'em!"

The five stopped working and glared at Hick. Turning to one another they shook their heads, shrugged and resumed their work.

Inside the ship, Hick found Hiroshi stacking boxes of video disks near the hatch. "What are you doing?"

"Dude, I wanted to lighten the ship for take off, so I decided to dump these disks. They're all Medieval fiction. I've seen them a million times and I'm sick of it. I've outgrown all that wizardry, jousting, swordplay and dragon stuff, and you were never into it anyway, so out they go!"

Hick nodded. "You're right." It's all pretty boring, dump it!"

The two men carried the boxes of disks away from the ship and stacked them neatly under a tree.

"I sure hate to litter like this." Hick looked at the surrounding landscape.

"Dude, environmentalists back on earth will never know." Hiroshi chuckled.

"I s'pose you're right." Hick joined with a laugh, recalling how Hiroshi had bombed Munchville with cow manure. *This could be no worse,* his expression sobered, *or could*   *it?*

Chapter Sixteen

Hick awakened on the sofa in the crew lounge wondering where he was and how he got there. Sleep had been fleeting, with questions of Roni's fate preoccupying his every toss and turn. He was further aggravated by the knocking sounds on the outer hull made by the munchipod drivers fueling the ship.

Rising to his feet, Hick stretched and yawned. He looked at the dog sleeping peacefully on the deck beside the couch and wished he could do the same. His every movement was drudgery as he prepared for the day.

Hiroshi had left a note saying he had gone to Munchville to purchase fresh fruit and vegetables, promising to meet Hick at the rodeo.

Hick locked Uggy Dog onboard the ship for safe keeping. After taking Bubba from the carnival exhibit to the rodeo chute, Hick climbed the fence to watch the calf roping and bull dogging. The laughter and applause of the crowd seemed distant. Even the newly installed big screens at both ends of the arena escaped his notice at first.

Clint mounted the fence and sat down by Hick. "The mayor has called for an emergency session of the town council to address certain improprieties, whatever that means. He says that greasing the bull's back is cheating, and that the riders are supposed to have a strap to hold onto. He's proposing that you and Hiroshi be hanged after the rodeo for cheating on your wager. He also says that the dance you introduced is far from modern. Guess that alien, Boo, told Wild Bill, and he told the mayor. So even if Wild Bill cuts a deal with you they won't live up to it."

Hick paid little attention to Clint's rambling, his mind was on Roni and the escape. He hardly noticed when Hiroshi climbed the fence beside him.

"Dude, did I miss anything exciting?"

Hick shook his head.

"Ladies and gentlemen, may I have your attention please?" the loud speaker blared, "there's been a change in today's program. Weasel will not be giving his exhibition today. Instead, Wild Bill is offering you a special treat performance by a new performer. Ladies and Gentlemen, if you look to the ends of the aisle you will see attendants handing out virtual goggles. Please take one and pass 'em down. Within minutes the entire crowd, with the exception of Hick and Hiroshi, had donned their goggles, and all eyes were focused on center arena.

"Ladies and Gentlemen, please welcome our Rodeo Queen, Charlotte.

A huge woman in a buckskin dress strode from an opening beneath the grandstands into the arena.

Hick noticed that the image projected on the big screen showed a well dressed, petite munchipod woman walking into the arena.

As the applause grew from average to an uproar, Hick felt his jaw drop. A cold sweat covered his forehead and pain shot through his abdomen.

"Wow, she's gorgeous," shouted Clint, almost losing his balance.

After catching Clint to keep him from falling, Hick removed his hat and goggles. "Take a second look," he said.

"Ugh!" Clint moaned and grimaced. "I can't believe I thought she was pretty!"

"Ladies and Gentlemen," the loudspeaker blared, "Charlotte is going to lead us in a chorus of 'Git along home Cindy-Cindy.'"

The music began to play. Charlotte sang off key, leaping, spinning and swaying, as the crowd swayed and do-si-doed, singing at the top of their lungs:

"Git along home Cindy Cindy
Git along home Cindy Cindy

Git along home Cindy Cindy,
I'll marry you someday"

Hick turned to Hiroshi. "Can you believe this?"

Hiroshi nodded. "Unusually agile for a big girl, isn't she?"

After the third chorus, Charlotte ended the song. She bowed to the audience. Then she waved and blew a kiss to Hick.

"Dude, don't tell me that is Thee Charlotte?" Hiroshi smiled.

"That's her!" Hick replied, adding, almost silently, "makes me want to take a bath and gargle.

*

As Charlotte made her exit beneath the grandstands, Wild Bill walked to the center of the arena. The loud speaker announced his entrance, "Ladies and Gentleman, Wild Bill has taken center arena to offer a deal to Mister Hick. Mister Hick, will you please proceed to the center of the arena?

Hick cast an uneasy glance at Hiroshi before he slid from the fence and walked slowly out to meet Wild Bill.

"What happened to Weasel last night?" Wild Bill demanded with a piercing glare.

Hick tapped his forehead with his palm. "Weasel? Oh yeah. He got his ass chewed."

"You want Varonico?"

"Varonico?" Hick squinted.

"You know, the woman, Varonico!"

Hick could feel Wild Bill's hateful penetrating gaze. "That depends," he lied.

"Depends on what?"

"On how much you want for her." Hick tried to sound casual and uncaring.

"Well here's the deal Alien." Wild Bill's lips curled into a filthy smirk. "First you fight Boo. If you win, I'll trade the

139

woman for the bull. If you lose, the bull and the woman are mine to do with as I please! Understood?"

Hick hesitated, trying to think of an alternative, but the hard expression on Wild Bill's face told him there was no other way. "All right, but you must promise not to harm her." He searched Wild Bill's eyes for a trace of honor but found none.

"You have my word, I won't touch a hair of her head." Chuckling, he turned and nodded to the announcer.

"Ladies and gentlemen, Mister Hick has agreed to fight Wild Bill's alien slave Boo. If Mister Hick wins he gets the alien slave woman. If he loses, the bull goes to Wild Bill, and Wild Bill will shoot the alien woman."

The crowd applauded.

"And now bring out the alien woman."

Wild Bill walked confidently to the east end of the arena to watch the fight.

A gate opened at the west end, and Roni, hands tied and blindfolded, was led into the arena by two of Wild Bill's men.

"Now bring out the alien, Boo," the announcer instructed.

The two helpers left the arena. Moments later they returned leading Bo on a leash and collar, his hands tied behind his back. He wore ragged pants and boots, his naked upper body was a collage of dirt and tattoos.

Wild Bill's men untied Bo's hands and removed the collar. He stretched, and rubbed his hands together vigorously while he glared at Hick.

Hick shrugged and forced himself to relax.

The crowd stood to their feet as Bo rushed forward. Hick drew several deep breaths, he raised his arms just above waist level and lifted his heels.

Ten feet away Bo drew back his arm with clenched fist, telegraphing his intention so deliberately that Hick wondered if it was a guise for something more tricky. At arm's length, Bo swung with all his weight. Hick ducked to his left, extending his right leg and hooking Bo's ankle. Rising abruptly, he followed with a backhand to Bo's ribcage. Bo stumbled and fell with a grunt. He glared at Hick with eyes full of rage and humiliation.

A roar of surprise and approval rose from the crowd.

"C'mon Bo." Hick motioned with his fingers and taunted with a smile. "I'm just gettin' started with you."

Bo pushed himself to his feet. Cautiously he moved within reach of Hick, throwing a roundhouse right followed by a left, and another right, narrowly missing with each. Frustrated, he straightened and glared. "C'mon," he flouted, motioning with his fingers.

Hick skipped forward, connecting with a left jab to Bo's nose. Bo pulled both hands in front of his face to cover. Hick shot in low, throwing his arms around Bo's legs, lifting and turning, hurling Bo to the ground.

The crowd roared.

Straddling Bo's chest, and cushioning his knees on the big man's biceps, Hick unleashed a flurry of punches to Bo's face. There was no strategy, no technique, just revenge. Bo's cries for mercy, muffled by Hick's blows, seemed only to fuel his rage. When the big man's body relaxed, Hick pushed himself to his feet. He felt regret mixed with satisfaction. Uncertain of which emotion he should embrace, he turned and watched Wild Bill approach from the east end of the arena, rifle in hand.

Dropping to one knee, Wild Bill opened the breach, and loaded his rifle. Fixing his gaze on Roni, he licked his thumb, wetted his sight, and raised the rifle to his shoulder.

Hick had to do something even if it was hopeless. Summoning all his strength, he rushed toward Wild Bill, shouting mindlessly at the top of his lungs.

From the corner of his eye, Hick saw a large red-brown form moving rapidly across the arena in Wild Bill's direction. The roar of the crowd alerted Wild Bill to Bubba's charge. He turned and took aim at the bull but it was too late. Bubba's horns caught, and hurled him twenty feet skyward, meeting him on the way down, thrashing, tearing, and goring him mercilessly.

Hick stopped and looked to his right. Hiroshi held the chute gate open. Smiling he flashed Hick a "thumbs up."

The angry crowd shook their fists and cried "foul!"

"Quick, over here!" Clint came from behind Hick leading two robotic horses. "Here, take these and hurry. They'll be comin' after you. I'll get the gate." He handed Hick the reins to one of the horses and ran towards Hiroshi with the other.

A bugle blasted *charge,* from somewhere in the grandstands.

"Form the posse!" The mayor's voice boomed from the loudspeaker.

Hick threw the right rein over the horse's mane and leaped into the saddle. "How do you make this thing go?"

"Stand up in the stirrup," Clint called over his shoulder, as he delivered the other horse to Hiroshi.

Hick leaned into the stirrup. The horse began to move forward. He reined towards Roni, placing more weight into the stirrups. The horse gained speed.

The bugle's persistent blasts sent chills up and down Hick's spine. He pulled back on the reins, bringing the horse to a stop beside Roni. Reaching down, he caught her under the arm and lifted her to a sidesaddle position in front of him. "Hang on!" he shouted.

"What, without hands?" she complained.

"Oh great!" He pressed the stirrups gently, hoping the horse's acceleration would not match his mood.

"Hurry up!" Clint held the gate open at the east end.

Hick clenched the left rein between his teeth, and worked the ropes loose from Roni's hands. The horse veered dangerously close to the fence, just as Roni pulled the blindfold from her eyes.

"Aaaaaaah, you're going to hit the fence!" She threw her arms around Hick's head, blocking his sight.

"Would you shut up and sit down?" He regained control of the reins with his left hand and straightened the horse. "Let me go, I can't see," he said in a muffled voice, her breast pressed tightly against his face. "Just get down a little!"

"Okay." She relaxed her hold and slid into the saddle.

"Dude, let's go." Hiroshi was waiting by the east gate. He Looked down at Clint. "One more favor, little dude. Turn the livestock lose. Let's create some confusion."

"You got it." Clint saluted, and rushed back into the arena.

Hick straightened his horse and leaned into the stirrups. The horse gained speed, as it passed through the gate, smoothing into a gallop that reminded Hick of a magic carpet ride. He held Roni close, and for the first time in months he felt complete. If they could make it to the ship and lift off, all would be well.

***

Bo stood to his feet and trudged across the arena. Finding a robotic horse, he prepared to mount, but a huge arm encircled him and hurled him to the ground. He glared bewildered at the large woman standing over him.

"This one's mine," she bellowed, as she mounted, adding, "I saw it first!" Leaning into the stirrups, she rode away.

Finding another horse, Bo pulled himself into the saddle and started toward the gate.

"Help me Boo! I command you! Make him stop!" *It sounded like Wild Bill, pleading, begging.* Stunned by the irony, Bo reined his horse to a stop. The bull was calmly chewing on Wild Bill's limbless torso.

"Boo, I've been good to you. I provided you with food and shelter. If it weren't for me think where you'd be now."

Bo paused to savor the moment. A smile formed on his face. He spat on the ground. "You wanted the bull, now you've got him, or he's got you! By the way, it's Bo, not

Boo." Standing in the stirrups, Bo reined toward the open gate and leaned forward bringing the horse to a full gallop.

*

"Dude, we have to hurry, the posse won't be far behind." Hiroshi entered the code and turned to Roni and Hick. "It will take a few minutes for the engines to power up and adjust to the fuel mixture, but I think I can bring us to a hover on auxiliary and get us out of reach."

As the hatch opened, Uggy Dog greeted them dragging her leash. Hiroshi slipped past the dog and headed for the cockpit.

"Move your ass, Uggy," Hick cautioned, ushering Roni in front of him while leading the horses through the hatchway. Hick nudged Roni and pointed. "Follow Hiroshi, see if he needs help."

Roni nodded and hurried down the passageway. "Come on Lucki," she called, but the dog ignored her.

After securing the horses, Hick hurried back to the hatch and pressed the "close" button. The sound of the engines rose from a mild hum to a roar. Uggy dog stood at the narrowing hatchway barking, as a rider, too large for the horse, approached at full gallop. The craft began to rock and vibrate, lifting slowly from the ground. A cloud of green dust stirred, partially obscuring the rider, but not enough to satisfy Hick. "Get back Uggy dog," he shouted as he pressed the "close" button repeatedly, wishing the hatch would shut faster. He knew Charlotte couldn't reach the hatch before it closed, he simply couldn't stand the sight of her, and if pressing the button more would buy a split second, then it was worth it.

Charlotte dismounted and rushed toward the ship. Only a crack of an opening remained in the hatch. Her muted screams of anger and despair sent chills down Hick's spine. Her fingers clawed and pried at the small opening, as the ship rose above her shoulders, then her head.

An alarm sounded, which Hick supposed was nothing more than a normal part of liftoff. With a glance, he realized Uggy Dog's leash was caught on the runner between the frame and the hatch, preventing it from closing.

Hick knew the ship could not take off with the door ajar, but it could hover. He tugged on the leash to no avail. The door had to go full cycle, it could not merely be opened a little.

He pressed the "open" button. Wind, dust and noise accelerated as the hatch slid open. The craft was only eight feet off the ground but rising slowly. Charlotte clung with white knuckles to the threshold. Her voice echoed above the noise, "You'll never leave me again!" Hick grabbed the leash and tugged, but it was stuck tight between Charlotte's hand and the threshold.

A second rider approached at full gallop, it was Bo. He leaped from the saddle, and gripped the threshold beside Charlotte. The two began punching, kicking and gouging one another, each clinging to the threshold with one hand.

Hick tried to pry Charlotte's fingers loose, but she reached up with her free hand and grabbed him by the collar. He lost his balance and somersaulted over the side, catching himself, and swinging from the hem of her buckskin dress. The ship was sixty feet off the ground and rising. *Letting go was not an option, and looking down was unraveling.* Above him, Bo and Charlotte continued their struggle, trading blow for blow. Uggy Dog peered over the side, carrying on frantically, every bark—a plea for Hick's safety.

If God had only put hands on Rottweilers. Hick began climbing Charlotte's dress. He was halfway up when the material ripped horizontally across Charlotte's midsection exposing her bare buttocks. Hick dropped several feet before the material stabilized. Ever-so-carefully he began to pull himself back up. When he reached Charlotte's buttocks, he found himself facing a large, pink, heart shaped tattoo, over a wall of cellulite, which read, "Charlotte and Hick, true love forever." The thought sent adrenaline pumping through his veins, and helped him climb with renewed vigor.

*

Hiroshi noticed the flashing red light on the console, "Hatch door open." He glanced at Roni. "Dude! Hick might be having some trouble. Here, take the stick, I'll go see what's going on."

Roni positioned herself in the copilot's seat, but hesitated, "What do I do?" she said with a quiver in her voice.

"Just hold it steady," he replied, taking her hand and placing it on the stick. "I'll be right back."

*

Hick had almost reached Charlotte's shoulders, when he noticed Hiroshi standing beside Uggy Dog. Hiroshi pulled the leash free from Charlotte's hand and stomped her fingers. Her screech vibrated above the noise and searing wind, as she gripped the threshold with her free hand.

Seizing the opportunity, Bo doled out unanswered blows, while Hiroshi stomped Charlotte's other hand.

"Not her," Hick shouted, "if she falls, I fall!" He pointed at Bo, "Him!"

"Dude! How'd ya' get down there?" Hiroshi shouted, shaking his head remorsefully, his hair flying wildly in the wind. He ceased stomping Charlotte's fingers and began stomping Bo's instead.

*

Roni held the stick like Hiroshi instructed. She was certain the hatch light was a minor problem, although she couldn't help but wonder what was taking Hiroshi so long. She calmed herself and released a sigh. *Everything was going*

146

to be fine. Then she heard a buzzing noise, the unmistakable sound of a bee, *a large green bee circling her head.* She swatted once, twice…

*

Hiroshi lost his balance and slipped over the side as the ship tilted. On his way down he latched onto Bo's leg with both hands and held tight.

"Now it's your turn, sucker," Bo shouted, glaring down, and kicking Hiroshi violently about the chest and shoulders with his free leg.

"Owe dude," Hiroshi groaned, nearly losing his hold on the big man's leg. In desperation, Hiroshi bit into Bo's calf, momentarily supporting himself with his teeth, while trapping Bo's other leg with his hands. Through clenched teeth he forced a muffled, "Still your turn, dude!"

Bo screamed in agony from the pain of Hiroshi's bite. His expression went from shock to a grimace accompanied by another scream, as Hiroshi grabbed crotch, pockets, anything he could use for a handle to climb Bo's body.

Charlotte resumed pummeling Bo with her free hand, while Hick climbed from her massive shoulders to the threshold, and with Uggy Dog's help, tugging on his shirt, he pulled himself through the hatchway.

Hick unsnapped the leash from Uggy Dog and motioned her back away from the opening. Tying one end of the leash to a hand rail on the outer hull, he tossed the other end to Hiroshi. "Grab hold," he shouted.

Hiroshi took the leash and released Bo's leg while Charlotte and Bo continued trading kicks and punches.

*

"Hold your fire," said the sheriff, "They've got Queen Charlotte!"

Members of the posse gasped in terror, as they watched Charlotte, through virtual goggles, dangling from the hovering spaceship.

"Quick, grab saddle blankets, bedrolls, whatever you got, gather 'round 'em and hold 'em up to cushion her in case she falls!" The sheriff shouted.

*

Battered and beaten, Bo's grip began to loosen. A final blow from Charlotte ended the fight. He grabbed repeatedly for Hiroshi, hanging securely from the leash. "I'll get you, ya' little Nip Bastard!" he threatened.

Dodging the big man's grasp, Hiroshi drew back his free hand in a fist. "Wait for it—wait for it! Hi-yah!" Hiroshi's sudden rabbit punch on Bo's nose, with, "Dude, that's Mister Nip Bastard to you!" caused Bo's eyes to roll back, and sent him plummeting ground-ward.

Hick pulled Hiroshi up, together they prepared to pull Charlotte to safety, but as they reached for her arm, she looked into Hick's eyes. "Goodbye my love," she said, releasing her hold.

The two men watched as Charlotte plunged, and landed flat on her back in a blanket supported by a circle of posse members. The force of her impact sent the posse flying in different directions.

"Ooooh!" Hick threw his hand over his eyes. "That's gotta' hurt."

Hiroshi's eyes enlarged "Dude, that was a ground shattering event!"

"Let's get out-a here," Hick suggested.

"I'm for that," Hiroshi agreed.

*

Munchville was like a ghost town with a breeze whistling down the dirt street.

Outward through the saloon's swinging doors walked a lone green figure. The heels of his cowboy boots tapped lightly on the board walkway and his spurs jingled.

Clenched tightly in his left hand was a half empty bottle of rot gut. A pair of six guns hung from his hips. He stepped from the walkway to the dirt street, and turned to his left, placing the sun at his back. Scarcely fifty feet in front of him stood his rival, poised and ready, his right hand cupped in preparedness beside his pistol, his large white hat towered above his head.

"Your move, Duke!" Clint offered calmly.

With lightning speed Duke drew the gun from his holster and fired, shooting the bottle from Clint's hand. The bottle ignited sizzling upward with a hissing noise before exploding in a loud bang high overhead.

Stepping forward, Clint drew the pistol from his right holster, spinning it skillfully and firing.

Duke's left arm was blown off at the shoulder, yet he continued, seemingly unaffected by the loss. He fired again striking Clint in the left leg.

The severed leg fell to the ground. Clint hopped forward on the remaining leg, spinning and shooting his pistols, each bullet finding its mark until silence fell again over Munchville.

Epilogue

The ship set down in a green grassy meadow surrounded by beautiful trees and a fresh running brook on a virgin planet. Hick and Roni disembarked along with Uggy Dog and the two cows while Hiroshi watched from the hatchway.

"We could build a cabin over on that knoll." Hick pointed. "And I could have my barn over there."

"No, that spot is reserved for my garden," Roni corrected. "You could put your barn over there."

"That tree would make a nice swing for the kids."

"That tree will make a wonderful swing for the kids," she agreed, leaning into his arms.

***

In the streets of Munchville two dismembered figures lay motionless side by side, a trail of severed arms and legs strewn behind each.

"What do you say we call a truce and be friends?" asked one.

"We'll shake on it as soon as our arms grow back," the other replied with a sigh.

***

"What is all this?" The sheriff pointed at the stack of boxes near the landing sight searching the hardened faces of his deputies for an answer.

"Those are video disks," Bo replied with a quick helpful tone from the back of a robotic horse, his hands bound behind him.

"Nobody told you to talk." The sheriff countered sharply.

"But I know where there's a video player. There's probably some interesting material in those boxes."

The sheriff rested on his saddle horn, scratching his chin and nodding. "Wonder what Queen Charlotte would say about that?"

THE END?
Perhaps

Special thanks to Jesus Christ, without whom I would be lost, My mother, Katherine, and my daughters, Jo Jo and Ilene for always believing in me.

What's Your Problem, Cowboy? Is a work of fiction. Any similarity of characters and events in this story to real people or events would be outrageous and hilarious.

Made in USA - Kendallville, IN
89158_9780970224705
03.18.2024 2337